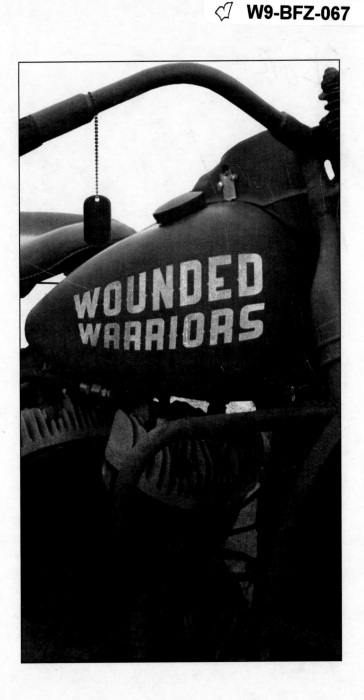

For

Mary

Love Elliott

2012

WOUNDED WARRIORS

Sam Wesst

TATE PUBLISHING
AND ENTERPRISES, LLC

Published by Tate Publishing & Enterprises, LLC
127 E. Trade Center Terrace | Mustang, Oklahoma 73064 USA
1.888.361.9473 | www.tatepublishing.com

Tate Publishing is committed to excellence in the publishing industry. The company reflects the philosophy established by the founders, based on Psalm 68:11,
"The Lord gave the word and great was the company of those who published it."

Book design copyright © 2012 by Tate Publishing, LLC. All rights reserved.
Cover design by Brandon Land
Interior design by Ranilo Cabo

Published in the United States of America

ISBN: 978-1-62024-794-5
FICTION / Action & Adventure
28.07.20

Introduction

The Vietnam War was escalating, and the United States was suffering losses much greater than expected. In an effort to win battles and regain the confidence of the American public, a plan was put into place to gather intelligence and cripple the enemy.

Special units of men were recruited from the Marine Corps and taken to undisclosed locations to be trained as super soldiers.

Declassified and considered non-combatants, these men were specially trained in mixed martial arts and weapons technology.

These units were sent behind enemy lines to gather intelligence, destroy targets, and eliminate any threat to the United States war effort.

Oftentimes these men worked with the CIA and other government agencies that did not acknowledge their existence.

A terrible truth about the war was being kept secret by these agencies and the men who worked as their operatives. The war at home had become very unpopular, and public protests were more common every day.

The special unit code name Ragged Eagles was allowed leave to return home to the United States for what could be their last time. This leave was granted before their next assignment, which would take them back to Southeast Asia. This would be the most dangerous and difficult mission they had ever encountered.

During their leave, they all rode their Harley Davidsons to the mountains in Mexico, where they formed a special bond with one another and planned their Broken Arrow mission.

A Fallen Friend
October 1975
Location: Ames, Iowa

The crowd was light, too light for the occasion. Jack mumbled under his breath. Dave had been a true loner for so long, the gathered bereaved must have been his family. How difficult it was coming back here. Jack glanced over, and a lovely, black dress adorning a young woman with beautiful, long, blonde hair caught his eye. Her handkerchief covered her face from her eyes to her mouth as she wept quietly.

Jack made brief eye contact with her as he walked by the pew and slowly stepped up to the casket. The casket was closed, and several pictures of Dave were adorned on top. One photo stood out in particular. It was a wooden-framed picture, larger than the others of Dave, and it showed Jack and all the guys from the unit. They were smiling and standing by their Harleys as they posed for the shot with the mountains of Mexico in the background. Displayed next to the picture were all of Dave's medals from Vietnam. Jack smiled as he remembered the trip and the day the photo was taken. So many good times were had on that trip. Unfortunately no more would be had, as Dave was gone. The finality of it hit Jack hard, taking his breath away.

Jack flinched as he felt a soft touch on his sleeve. He looked over to see the young, blonde woman in the black dress looking into his eyes. She too was still shedding tears. Her lips were quivering, and her hands trembled a bit as she said, "Jack?"

Puzzled, Jack looked in her blue eyes and said, "I'm sorry, do I know you?"

"Yes, you do," she said in a confirming but confused voice. "It has been many years. I'm Terri."

Jack, still puzzled, said, "Terri?"

"Yes. Terri Thompson, Dave's sister."

"Oh God, of course you are." He reached out and pulled her into his embrace. How could this beautiful woman be the same little girl he had known long ago when he first came home with Dave, while they had been on leave? She leaned in and began to sob softly against his chest. Jack comforted her and held her tight, hoping to take some of the burden off of her. Even now, after all these years, he still wanted to protect her.

A deep pain set in next to Jack's heart. He swallowed hard, trying to hold his emotion in check. He took her hand. "Let's walk outside for some fresh air."

She took his hand and laid her head on his shoulder. They walked out the front door and stood off to the side, allowing the few who were there for the funeral to go inside. The quietness of the day and their hearts was disturbing. Jack, feeling the awkwardness, decided to break the torment that was eating at his heart and mind. "Terri," he said, "I have to ask. What did Dave do when he got back home?"

"Nothing—nothing at all. He drank excessively and smoked pot like it was going out of style. That was all we could get him to do."

Jack looked down and let out a moan. "Oh dear God."

"The whole family tried getting him job after job, and he would never show up for the interviews, so they all gave up on him. My father even tried starting businesses with him, trying to help him out and show him he could be good at something else, but it all fell apart. He was getting very strange toward the end. I can't put my finger on it, but he was never the same. No one could figure out what was going on with him.

"Sometimes I would go over to his apartment where my folks let him stay, and I would knock, but he wouldn't answer. So I would walk in, and I'd find him blindfolded cleaning his gun. He never would acknowledge me. He would just keep assembling and disassembling that gun over and over. It was like he was in his own world. We physically got him back, but mentally he was never really the same."

The minister came out of the church and stood next to them. As he held the big, wooden doors open, they could hear the organ playing in the background.

"Excuse me, folks, the service is about to begin. Please come and find your seats," he said. The small group of people that had gathered outside the doors put out their cigarettes and walked into the church.

Jack took Terri's arm and escorted her back into the church. Glancing to his left, he saw three men in full dress uniforms as they saluted him. A sad smile came across his face, and he saluted back, accepting their nods as they said, "Sir." Jack and Terri walked down the aisle to their seats and saw five more men in civilian clothes, and as the recognition was immediate, they exchanged nods. The service started with the standard prayers, and the formalities were conducted. Jack, trying to hold his emotions, looked over and saw Dave's parents with anguish and almost a sense of relief apparent on their faces. Dave's father recognized him immediately and smiled. Quietly he reached over and shook Jack's hand while tears filled his eyes, and gave him a nod in acknowledgement.

The service continued, and Jack tried to focus, but the memories of Dave were too overwhelming. Jack brought his attention back to the service as the minister began the eulogy and welcomed others to share their stories of Dave. A few family members addressed the congregation. Laughs were exchanged, and truthful moments were shared to remember and celebrate Dave's life.

After the service, the local Honor Guard and Dave's relatives moved the casket out of the church to the awaiting hearse. Dave's parents followed the casket, followed by Jack and Terri. Jack walked slowly with Terri, holding her as she continued to sob. The day was somber, as was the event. Terri led Jack to the limousine and asked him to join her for the ride to the gravesite.

The cemetery was a beautiful place high on a hill that overlooked a meadow. One could see the river running through it and the row of great pine trees on either side. It was a beautiful place to be laid to rest. *Finally,* Jack thought, *Dave can be at peace here.*

Jack noticed the old headstones as he and Terri walked together to the cemetery plot. He saw all generations of Thompsons, one after the other. He couldn't help but think, *It's okay, Dave. You're home now. They are here for you.*

The graveside service was short, as was Dave's life. The Honor Guard fired their guns for Dave one last time, and the bugler played "Taps." Terri leaned over and hugged the casket and kissed it one last time and whispered, "Good-bye, my dear brother. May your worries be gone and your heart be full of love." Jack helped her up, and as they turned, three uniformed marines from Jack's first unit saluted the casket. The flag was then rolled corner to corner and was presented to Dave's parents.

They remained at the gravesite until all had left. As they turned to walk back to the limousine, they saw that the men from the unit were all gathered around. Red, the biggest guy of the bunch, said, "We must tip the bottle for Dave tonight!"

"Yes!" agreed Jack. "Where do you guys want to meet?"

Terri, with her spirit suddenly lifted and always the one to be on her brother's side, said, "O'Malley's! Oh, Dave loved it there!"

"Right, O'Malley's Pub it is. How about six p.m.—I mean, 1800 hours?"

They all smiled and in unison said, "Yes, sir," and they all headed toward their cars.

Jack and Terri rode in the limo back to the church for the ceremonial sandwiches, goodies, and coffee. There was a lot of chatter as the room was filled with friends and family reliving memories of Dave when he was a little boy. Listening to all of the stories made Jack a little uneasy, and, not able to stand it a minute longer, he felt the need for some fresh air to clear his head. He searched out Terri. "How 'bout we go for a walk? I need to clear my head."

Instinctively, Terri grabbed her purse and kissed her mother and father and let them know that they were going to step outside for a bit.

Outside, the crisp air was a welcome distraction. Terri said, "Do you remember when all you guys came home from boot camp with Dave instead of going home to your own families?"

"Yes," said Jack with a laugh. "Our families were so pissed off."

Terri laughed—one of those deep laughs that hit a person right at their core, throwing Jack a bit off guard. "Remember how my mom gasped when the whole bunch of you showed up on the step with Dave, and he's like, 'Hi, Mom, I'm home.' Oh God, the look on her face, it was wonderful."

"Yeah, your folks were great. Still are. They took us all in and gave us a bed and a shower just like we were their own kids. The hell they must be going through now."

"Yeah. We were all so frightened for you guys. My mom went to church every day until you guys got home. She just knew that if she prayed hard enough and long enough you would all return safely."

"Wow," said Jack, "I didn't know that she was so religious."

"Yeah, even my dad was praying. There were times when I remember coming down the steps and I would see him sitting at the kitchen table. He must have been praying because in his left hand he had a Bible and in his right hand, a cup of coffee. He would just be sitting there staring out the window."

"Wow," said Jack, "I didn't know that your dad even went to church."

"He doesn't really, but I think he does have a true relationship with God. Do you know what I mean, Jack?"

"Yes, I do. I can relate that way." Jack paused and collected his thoughts for a moment, trying to understand the toll war took on the mind and body. "Your Father was a World War II vet, right?"

"Yes. He was in the Battle of the Bulge."

"Amazing…"

"He never talks about it though. It's as if it's a part of his life that we know happened but that he tries to forget."

"Understandable," said Jack. "Those guys went through hell over there. A hell that you and I can't even imagine, and I think they'd rather we not even have to try to understand."

Reserved, Terri said, "Yes, I think that was why he is so quiet and distant at times. It did something to him."

"Yeah, it would. I think the right thing to do is to respect his privacy and not ask questions. When he's ready, he'll talk. He may never get there, but you have to give him the space and time to do so if he chooses."

They continued to walk along the river, and the sun was shining, and the leaves on the trees rattled as the breeze softly blew and gently ran through her hair. Terri said, "Dave came back so different. What really happened to him, Jack?" They stopped, and Terri turned toward him and held his hands tight.

"Oh, Terri, you don't really want to know what happened over there. Trust me on that."

She just sighed and held his arm tight as they continued to walk along a pathway covered with autumn leaves.

They came to a concrete bench placed along the pathway and sat down. Terri sat close to him, close as if trying to hold on to a part of something she might never get back. Jack leaned forward and closed his hands around hers, and she laid her head on his shoulder.

For the two of them, it was as if time had stood still for a brief moment—just held in limbo, with nowhere to go. Terri whispered, "We should go soon. The guys will be waiting for you at the pub."

"Yeah," he said, "let's lighten the mood little. I think Dave would have wanted that."

"I think you're right," she said as she looked up at him and smiled. They slowly walked back to the church. Terri lifted her face to the warm sun and noticed a beautiful bald eagle soaring across the top of the trees. She whispered to herself, "You're free, Dave. Go in peace."

Saluting a Comrade

O'Malley's Pub was a place like no other. The smell of stale beer and peanuts could keep you coming back for more. Jack and Terri walked in and noticed that the guys were feeling no pain. Red and Ringo were already in some kind of a drinking contest as they walked in, and the other guys were cheering them on as they chugged down beers.

Jack walked to the bar and ordered a round for everyone. As he waited for his order, he glanced around and saw the chair in the center of the room with Dave's jacket, hat, and dog tags hanging on the back. What a sad sight. This just wasn't right.

Donnie Roscoe was not celebrating. He had lost one of his closest friends. Silently, he walked to the chair and put his hand on Dave's jacket and gently rubbed the collar, remembering all the good times they had. Jack joined him and in a soft whisper said, "Donnie, you know that Dave's in a better place now. His battles are finally over."

Donnie replied in a scratchy and remorseful voice, "Man, I hope so. Captain Jack, we sure went through some real heavy stuff, didn't we?"

"Yeah," Jack said, "heavy is an understatement." Donnie nodded in agreement.

"Come on, let's have a drink."

"Sure," he said, "but ice water is fine."

Jack turned and looked at him. "Is that how you snipers keep a steady hand on the trigger? By drinking ice water?"

Donnie grinned, "I'll maybe have a drink later. Right now I want to stay alert."

Jack, puzzled by this statement, said, "Are you all right, Donnie?"

"Yeah, sure. I'm all right." Then he looked up and paused. "Let's join the others. We don't want to disappoint Dave."

Jack and Donnie walked back to the group and could see that the beers were backing up on the table in front of them. There was a shot in everyone's hand, and they all raised their glasses as Jack shouted, "A toast to US Marine Dave Thompson, who fought, defended, honored, loved, and gave freedom to this ground."

They all raised their glasses a little higher and shouted in unison, "United States of America! Hoo-yah!" And they all downed the shots of whiskey.

Jack then shook hands with the men, each one of them telling him a little story about Dave. Jack, not knowing what to do with all the attention, turned and said, "It's damn good to see each and every one of you."

He then turned to Terri, and said, "At ease, men. You all should remember Terri, Dave's little sister."

She slapped Jack hard on the shoulder. "Little! Who the hell do you think you are talking to? Little sister my ass!"

Raising his glass of beer, Jack said, "Let me rephrase. I mean, the younger sister!"

"His younger sister! My God, I am a grown woman! Maybe if you hadn't been gone so long you would have been here to see that I am all grown up." She stood up straight and accentuated her chest. At this, the marines gave out a loud hoot and whistles that were heard throughout the bar.

Laughing, Jack held Terri's hand as she sauntered over to a barstool. Her tight, long, black dress gave her some trouble as she sat down. When she did, her slender thigh was peeking out of the long slit on the side, and all eyes were on her and that sexy slit in her dress. Jack leaned over and said, "What's your pleasure, my lady?" Be it the liquor or the state she found herself in, she blushed and requested a beer.

"Well, okay, beer for the pretty lady!"

"Hey, Jack, go get the beer and stop undressing me with your eyes."

"That obvious, huh?"

"Yes," she said, "but I don't mind. I appreciate the attention." Jack chuckled nervously, and a couple of the guys overheard them and started to laugh.

Good times, thought Jack. *Dave would have loved this.* Jack looked over and saw a couple of plain-clothed guys—suits probably.

The guys were sitting quietly at a table in the corner, drinking beer. It was as if they were supposed to be there but weren't invited. Jack couldn't help but notice the military-style watch, earpiece, and glasses. Slowly Jack walked to the men's room, contemplating his next move. As if anticipating Jack's thoughts, Ringo walked in and stood at the stall next to him. Jack had given him the name of Ringo in boot camp, and it had stuck ever since. They all thought he had looked like Ringo Starr, if Ringo would have had a buzz cut.

Ringo said, "Who are they? Feds? Special ops? Spooks?"

Quietly, Jack responded, "Spooks, I think. They could be others. Not quite sure at this moment. I was a bit caught up in Terri to notice them from the get-go. I missed it when I walked in. Must mean I'm losing my touch."

Ringo, ignoring Jack's comment, responded, "What do they want?"

"Who knows? Maybe we should invite them to the party."

"That's a good idea. Right smart. It would only be neighborly to do so!"

"Yeah," said Jack. They washed their hands, combed their hair, and walked out of the men's room and headed toward them. Jack motioned to the waitress to bring him two beers. Jack and Ringo got to the table just as the waitress arrived with the drinks.

"Evening, gents! What brings you to these parts?" Jack raised his voice so it was loud enough to get the attention of the others in the bar. The guys looked genuinely uncomfortable with the attention that was being directed at them. As Jack continued to talk, they began to fidget a bit.

Jack reached out his hand and said, "Jack Monroe, and you are?" The first guy introduced himself as Neil and shook Jack's hand.

"Well, Neil, you got a last name?"

"Young, Neil Young."

"Right," said Jack, "and you?" He turned and looked at the other guy sitting at the table.

"Yeah, my name is Dennis."

"And what's your last name, Dennis?"

"Hopper," he said, "Dennis Hopper."

"Okay now, we have a couple of famous guys here, Ringo. I'd like you to meet Dennis Hopper and Neil Young." He looked Neil in the eye. "Are you guys lost?"

They looked at each other, but Neil didn't answer.

Forcefully, Jack said, "Are you lost?"

"Oh, ah, no!" They started to fumble inside their suit coats.

Jack and Ringo leaned forward, and in a low voice, Jack demanded, "Don't even think about it. Don't unsnap those holsters on the guns you are packing unless you want them shoved right up your ass!"

The two gentlemen were motionless. "Who are you guys?" demanded Jack. "Feds? Military? Or spooks? Answer me!" he shouted.

The whites of their eyes got bigger, and Jack said, "I see. Maybe you are black ops spies following ex-combat guys around? What's the matter? You afraid Dave's ghost is going to walk through the door and shoot you in the head? Or are you worried these guys are going to share some info with that drunken farmer sleeping in the booth over there?"

Again, they looked puzzled, and yet they didn't speak. The air was thick, almost suffocating. Jack looked at Ringo and said, "They're here to report and observe. Or is it the other way around? Either way, go report to your superior officer. Operation crosstalk has started! All these guys are planning a covert operation for the Russians. We are going to take over all the farm co-ops and hold the grain hostage. No food for Americans, only exports to Russia!"

The guy that called himself Dennis Hopper made the first move and stood up. "Funny asshole." He threw a twenty-dollar bill on the table. Neil stood, following the lead of Dennis, and shook his head. As they walked out with their backs to the crowd, Jack yelled out, "Don't come back now! While you're here in town, maybe you guys should be disguised as scarecrows or cows! You'd be sure to blend in better than you are right now." Ringo and Jack exchange a quick glance, and Jack noticed the whole bar was completely silent, mouths agape, as they all tried to comprehend what had just occurred.

A moment or two passed, and the whole bar burst into laughter—that is, everyone but Terri. Getting up from the table, Jack eyed her and mouthed, "Don't worry," and began to move toward her. As he was making his way across the bar, the guys began questioning him, still looking for the direction he had always provided. As he made his way toward Terri, he was bombarded with questions. Jack, addressing the comrades, stated, "I am not sure who they were. Black ops, spooks, may be assassins? Damn straight I'm gonna find out what they hell they're up too."

Jack leaned into Terri, resting his hand on her back and trying to comfort her as she blurted out, "Oh God, are you serious?"

Sensing her frustration and uneasiness, he tried to comfort her. "No, they are just some dumbass FBI agents who were instructed to put a tail on us."

"Are you sure? I mean how do you know, Jack?"

Smiling, Jack looked her in the eyes. "Gray suit, white shirt, black tie, wingtips, Timex watch with a military band, earpieces, and no military training."

"How do you know they have no military training? How can you be so sure?"

"They let me get in their face with their weapons still holstered, and they looked like they were gonna piss their pants right there. My guess is they are college kids fresh out of Dumb Dumb Academy."

"Wow," said Terri, "you really know this stuff!"

Jack said, "I lived it overseas. They may as well have driven into town with a flashing neon sign on their car that said brand new FBI agents. If these guys were the real deal and wanted us quiet for some reason, they would have taken us out at the funeral. They wouldn't have come onto our turf."

"Oh God," said Terri. "What are they after? Why would they be here?"

"Not sure yet, but they are supposed to watch us for some reason. My guess is someone else is trying to figure something out or they assume we know too much. They need to back off if they know what's good for them."

Terri sat there silent and looked at him confused. Jack could sense it was becoming too much for her. She had just buried her brother with questions unanswered, and now there were more unanswered questions. He got up from the table and headed toward the guys by the pool table. Terri, not wanting to be alone, followed him as he moved through the bar. The others were still putting down the beer, not concerned with what had just taken place. It wasn't in Jack's nature not to worry—too much of his life had revolved around worrying and not trusting. With Terri's hand on his back, Jack looked at his watch and said, "I think I should make my way to the hotel and check in."

All the guys were drinking heavily, shouting, saluting each other, and bragging about girls, cars, and how tough they were in high school. Just like the old times. The bar had returned to its natural state of foul smell and chaos. Jack said, "Hey, guys, don't hang out too late. Tomorrow is sure to get here!"

"Yeah, yeah." They all laughed. "Hey come on, Jack, don't go. Let's party like rock stars!"

"Man, I never was a rock star, and I really don't need to party like one tonight anyway."

Terri looked at Jack and smiled. Her blue eyes were damp again.

"Walk me home, Jack." She took his hand, and as they walked out, a few of the guys stopped what they were doing and watched them. Jack was a man of many talents, and somehow he always ended up with the girl, no matter what the situation.

As they walked along a quiet sidewalk, Terri, holding Jack's arm to steady herself, said, "Jack, Dave loved you very much."

"I know. You told me. No need to tell me again. We all feel the same about him."

Terri let her tears fall, and no additional words were needed. The night was so quiet and still, and soon they came to the hotel on Main Street.

Jack said, "Let me check in, and then I'll walk you to the house."

"It's only ten blocks from here, Jack. I can walk."

"Well, wearing that tiny, little dress, you could freeze something off."

Terri smiled as she told Jack to check in.

Jack said, "I'll be right back, and then we can discuss that more, okay?" As he walked into the hotel, Jack realized Terri was a bit more drunk than he thought. Maybe it wouldn't be a bad idea for her to stay. As he entered the hotel, he heard her yell, "I just want to cuddle up with you." Jack shook his head and continued walking, thinking what his plan of action should be.

When Jack returned with the key, Terri followed him to his room. Jack unlocked the door and before he could even get the key out, Terri walked around him and pushed it open and walked into the room.

"I'll wait right here." She sat down on the bed. Jack put down his bag and turned to look at Terri. No longer was she sitting upright on the bed. There she was, lying flat on her back, passed out. He shook his head and sighed, knowing that he now had company for the rest of the night.

Jack pulled the covers back to prepare her for bed. He slipped off her shoes and dress, picked her up, and laid her down beneath the covers. He stopped and looked at her for a moment, taking in all her glorious features, wondering if she understood how truly blessed she was. Gently he kissed her on the forehead, pulled the covers up a bit, and turned out the light. He picked up the phone and called her parents. "Hi, I'm sorry to call so late, Mr. Thompson. Terri had too much to drink tonight and is going to crash at the hotel."

"Okay, Jack, but you keep the boys away from her."

"Don't worry, sir. I am right here with her."

"Okay, good night, son."

Jack put down the receiver and looked over at Terri. She was out cold and snoring like a bull moose. Standing there he thought about Dave and how he wished he could've protected him like this. He walked over to the cabinet and grabbed an extra pillow and blanket and tossed them on the floor. As he lay down, he thought, *It's okay, Dave. I'll watch over her for you now.* His eyes became heavy, and off he nodded.

A Time to Step Back

The sun was shining through the curtains when Jack began to stir the next morning. He rolled over and felt around for his watch. Picking it up, he looked at the time. It was already a little past eight a.m., and for a second, he began to panic. Being late was the one thing he despised. Finally he gained his senses and remembered that he was on vacation. He laid his head back down, took a deep breath, and stretched. After a few moments of realizing that sleep was not possible, he pulled himself up off of the floor and looked over at the bed, but it was empty. Terri was already up and gone. She had left a note on the pillow.

Jack,

Thank you for taking care of me last night. Please come by my parents' house today so I can thank you personally. I want to see you.

Terri

As Jack folded the note, he noticed a red mark in lipstick. "Ah, she has left a kiss for me," he said softly.

Jack smiled and walked to the shower and turned it on. As the water ran down his body, he thought of Dave and started to feel the emotions well up inside him again. He ducked his head under the spray of the shower and faintly heard the phone ring. He left the water running and stepped out of the bathroom, grabbing a towel on the way. He wrapped the towel around his waist and ran to the phone, water dripping on the carpet as he went.

"Jack?" the voice asked on the other end.

"Yeah. Who is this?"

"Ringo."

"Hey, what's up, Ringo?"

"Donnie is dead!" His voice was anxious.

"What? Donnie Roscoe! Hold on a sec—I just talked to him when I left the bar last night!"

"Yeah," Ringo said, "I did too!"

"What happened to him?"

"Car accident."

"Didn't he ride with you to the funeral and back to the hotel?"

"Yeah, he did, but he took the rental car when we got back to the hotel. He said he wanted to go to the bottle shop and get some brew for later."

"Was he drunk when he left?"

"No way, man. He only had a few. I know because we were all ripping him about it. He was the only one who wasn't putting them away."

"How the hell did he have an accident? Where was he?"

"Not sure, man, but I wanted to make sure you knew what was going on," Ringo replied.

Jack's mind was going a mile a minute. How did this happen? This was the last thing any of them needed right now.

"Where did they take him?"

"I was told he was at a hospital morgue here in town."

"What about the car? Where did they take that?"

"It's at the police impound lot in town, I think. They wouldn't give me much information."

Jack said, "Do any of the other guys still have a car?"

"Yeah, but where is your rental, Jack? Can't we just take that?"

"I left it at the bar last night when Terri and I walked to the hotel."

"Okay," he said, "I'll get another car and swing by and pick you up."

"All right, I'll be waiting. We gotta figure this out." Jack hung up the phone and sighed. "We've got to figure this out." He walked back into the bathroom and turned off the water in the shower, and then he pulled on a sweatshirt and some jeans. Sitting on the edge of the bed, he closed his eyes and started running possible scenarios through his head. He didn't like the coincidence of what had happened. It was just too much for one weekend.

After an hour of pacing and thinking, he was convinced that someone or something had caused Donnie's death. *This was no accident,* he thought to himself, *and those two suits at the bar last night are working for some-body who must know what happened.* Jack decided then and there that he would have to find out who they were and whom they worked for.

He went into the bathroom and brushed his teeth. He was combing his hair when he heard a knock at the door. He grabbed his .45 out of his leather bag and clicked off the safety. Slowly he walked to the door and stood off to the side and yelled, "Who is it?"

"Ringo!" a voice said from the other side.

Jack clicked the safety back on the gun and flipped the lock, pulled the chain off, and opened the door. Ringo walked in looking like he had been ridden hard and put away wet. Jack looked into his bloodshot eyes and said, "Hey, are you going make it there, partner?"

"Yeah, I'm all right," he scoffed with a tired and scratchy voice. "Let's Roll! This has turned into more than I thought I'd have to deal with this weekend."

Jack grabbed his leather shoulder holster and put it on and shoved a .45-caliber gun in each side. He picked up his leather jacket and slid it on. He then reached into his bag and found some extra clips, made sure they were full, and put them in the side pockets of his jacket. Ringo looked at him with a confused smile, and Jack said, "What, you're not packing?"

"Yeah sure, and back up is in my bag," he said.

"Good," Jack said. "Maybe your training will pay off!"

Again with a scratchy voice, Ringo said, "We'll see, Captain. We will see."

Jack grinned at him, and they both and walked out of the room, Jack locking the door behind him. They walked to the rental car. Ringo got behind the wheel and started it up. He put it into gear and drove up to the highway, the car throwing gravel off the rear wheels as they went. Once the tires hit the pavement, Ringo punched the accelerator hard. The weather had changed overnight, and it was now much colder. The wind had picked up, and the snow flurries were swirling around the car, and the exhaust pipe was leaving a vapor trail as they sped down the county highway.

As Jack and Ringo drove toward the hospital, Jack looked at Ringo and said, "Was it snowing or cloudy last night?"

"No," he said, "it was nice, very calm, and the stars were out, maybe a little cool but clear."

"Yeah," said Jack, "the stars were out in the Iowa sky."

Jack was silent the rest of the way. He just looked out the window as they sped down the highway. Ringo looked over at him occasionally but knew better than to speak because when Captain Jack was thinking it meant something was going to happen.

They pulled into the general parking area at the hospital and followed the sign that marked the route to the morgue. They parked the car and remained silent as they walked into the lobby. The hospital lobby was full of people—moms with their crying kids, elderly people confused as to where they were supposed to go, sick people looking for someone to help them. Jack and Ringo walked through the lobby following the signs to the morgue. They approached the morgue's desk that was manned by a young woman. She was wearing hospital blues and a nametag that read, "Amy/Morgue."

She looked up and asked, "Can I help you, sirs?"

"Yes, ma'am, my loved one is dead, and we were told he was here."

"Oh, I am sorry. Are you family or a friend?"

"Why do you ask?" said Jack.

"Because only family can view the body."

"Really, well, isn't that interesting. It's a good thing we're his cousins."

Amy grinned and said, "Yeah. Okay, what was the name of the deceased?"

"Donald Roscoe. He was brought here last night from a car accident."

"Just a moment please." She punched some numbers into the computer waited a moment and said, "Okay. Yes, he is here, but you're not going to be able to see the body right now."

Becoming frustrated, Jack asked why.

Amy took a step back from the counter and replied, "Because you have to be accompanied by the examiner. It's the rule here, not much I can do about it."

"Well, where is the examiner?"

"Not sure exactly. He left to run an errand some time ago. It's Sunday, you know, and they don't work all the time."

Jack took a breath said, "I know."

"Amy, could you please show him to us?"

"Okay, but you realize I can't tell you much other than the obvious."

"Because the examiner is not here?" said Jack.

"No," she said, "because the actual autopsy isn't scheduled until his next of kin have been notified. They have to approve the examination. It's state law."

Ringo leaned forward on the counter, trying to get a feel for the lady behind the desk. "Have you tried to contact them?"

"Yes," she responded, "but we don't seem to have information for any of them."

Jack looked at Ringo and then back at her and said, "Well, why don't you just let us see him for a moment? Then we'll get you the contact information for his next of kin."

She hesitated, but Jack smiled at her and said, "We are not going to touch anything, promise. We just want to make sure it's him."

She looked around and then back at Jack, and as their eyes connected, she smiled. "Okay, follow me." She took them into the cold, refrigerated room and opened a drawer that had a series of numbers on it.

As she pulled the drawer open, she looked at Jack again and said, "Are you sure?"

"Yes, I'm sure."

She unzipped the black body bag and pulled it back. Jack looked down at Donnie, then over at Ringo. He had his head down and was shaking it from side to side. Shock struck both of them, as they couldn't figure out what had happened.

"Donnie, what happened last night?" Ringo said.

"Look at all the bruises on his face," Jack said, "and it also looks like his nose is broken."

Jack looked at Amy. "Are there bruises on the rest of his body?"

"Well…" She hesitated. "You know I'm not supposed to say anything without the examiner, but yeah, unofficially, his knuckles are broken. He must have been in one hell of a fight before the car accident."

Anger began to creep into Jack's veins He had a deep look in his eyes and said, "Amy, what are they saying was the cause of death?"

"I can't tell you that now. It's not official without the—"

Jack said, "I know, without the examiner." He looked at her and said, "Okay, what's your personal opinion, off the record?"

"Well…" She paused again. "Head trauma. Someone hit him in the head so hard with a blunt object it most likely killed him or at least knocked him unconscious, and then he died."

Jack said, "Do you have an idea what the blunt object may have been?"

"Most likely a pipe or maybe the butt of a gun," she said. "Do you see this damage on his temple?" She pointed to the wound in his head.

"Yeah," Jack said.

"They intended to kill him when they hit him there, but it looks like he fought like hell to the death," she said.

"When is the autopsy supposed to occur?" Jack asked.

"Monday if we can notify his next of kin."

"Okay, Amy. Thanks. I'll be sure to get the number for you. I have it in my luggage. Do you need to call them directly, or can I do it for you?"

"Unfortunately, I have to have verbal confirmation from the next of kin."

Jack and Ringo thanked her and walked out of the morgue to the car. Disbelief was beginning to sink in. They looked at each other, and Jack said, "Are you thinking what I'm thinking?"

Ringo said, "Yeah, I am. I think we need to make a trip to the impound lot ASAP!"

Jack said, "Did he get all beat to hell from the car accident or not?"

"No way, man! Those bruises can't be from the accident," Ringo insisted.

They drove down Main Street and pulled into the sheriff station. Jack got out of the car and walked into the station and asked the desk sergeant where the impound lot was.

"Out back," he responded. "What can I help you with?"

"Did you bring in a car from an accident last night?"

"Yeah, sure did. It's a red Ford sedan, rental car, I think."

"Yeah," said Jack, "that's it."

The sergeant looked at Ringo for confirmation. "Yes, that was it," he said.

"Can we see it?" said Jack.

"Sure," the desk sergeant said. "The insurance agent was here this morning and went through everything, and I mean everything. Didn't have a much respect for anything that was in there. The rental company isn't going to be happy when they get here and see the shape the inside of the car is in."

"Really," said Jack. "That's odd. It usually takes them a few days to even show up, doesn't it?"

"Yeah, typically," he said. "I thought it was a little strange that he was here at seven in the morning with rubber gloves and a plastic bag. He tore the hell out of that car and all for an insurance rental car investigation. Seems a little strange to me."

"Did he ask about the accident at all?" Jack questioned.

"No," said the desk sergeant, "he never said a word about it. He just pulled the car apart."

"Did he mention the driver or the fact that it was a fatal accident?"

"No, he didn't, matter of fact. He just ripped the car apart."

Jack said, "Can you walk us back to the car?"

"Yeah, sure, let's go." They walked out back by miscellaneous junk cars, and Jack mentioned that some of the cars looked like they had been there for many years. "I guess that's small town USA." Ringo nodded in agreement.

They came up to the spot where the newer cars had been brought in. The car sat there intact except for a smashed front end, and the hood was folded back slightly. Jack told the sergeant, "Not very much damage for a car accident that killed somebody."

The sergeant looked at Jack and said, "Sometimes it doesn't take much though."

Jack asked who the officer was at the scene last night. As he walked around the car with Ringo, they looked at the door panels and noticed that the carpeting had been torn out and the front seat had been pulled out. The cushions were cut apart, and the foam stuffing had blown all over the lot.

The sergeant said, "Let me go back and find out who was on duty last night. I will be right back."

Ringo kneeled down and looked under the car. "Hey, what's this under the car?"

Jack knelt down and looked as well. He said, "What the hell! It's full of corn stocks and field grass! This thing went through a field, and looking at the dents underneath it—the exhaust was ripped up and bent—it almost looks like a chase."

"Yeah," Ringo said, "definitely a chase through a field."

Jack said, "So Donnie hit his head so hard it killed him. What side of his face was that on again?"

"The right, I think."

Jack said, "Look at the driver's compartment. Everything looks normal. So if he hit his head, what did he hit it on?"

Jack walked around and noticed the mirror, steering wheel, and shifter. They all looked normal—no dents, no breaks, no blood, nothing. He pulled down the sun visor, and it looked like the day it had come from the factory.

Confused, Jack said to Ringo, "Do you think this guy who was claiming to be the insurance investigator was looking for something?" Jack held up a car door panel that was completely ripped off.

Ringo shook his head and said, "Gee, why do you say that?"

Jack pulled the back door open and saw that the back seat also was torn apart, and the floor mats and carpeting were pulled up off the metal floor. Something definitely wasn't right. Whoever the investigator was, he wasn't there to investigate a rental car accident.

Just then, the desk sergeant walked back out and gave Jack a piece of paper. "Here is the number of Sergeant Davis, who was on duty last night. Davis is off today, so I made a call, and it's okay if you want to call the home number. Are we done here? I have to lock the gate up."

"Where exactly did the accident take place anyway?" said Jack.

"Edge of town, I think. I really don't know. It will be in the report, but it takes a few days to file it, you know. Davis will be able to answer those questions and any others you may have."

"Yeah, thanks," Jack said, and he and Ringo walked out and got into the rental car.

As they were driving away, Jack looked over at Ringo. "Edge of town must be out on the main highway somewhere, don't you think?"

"I don't follow."

"Consider this: They were driving on the edge of town, and they hit something or someone. There was no significant damage, but Donnie supposedly hits his head so hard he dies."

Ringo said, "No way could that happen, Jack. No way. It doesn't add up. What do you say we go see Sergeant Davis?"

"Yeah, there must be a pay phone around here where we can make a call."

Ringo pulled over to a roadside phone booth. Jack got out, pulled a dime out of his pocket, and dialed the number he was given.

The phone rang, and a woman answered. "Hello."

"Hi, I'm Jack Monroe, and I'm looking for Sergeant Davis. Is he home?"

"This is Sergeant Davis."

Jack was a bit surprised and said, "I'm a friend of the man who was killed in the accident last night."

"Oh, yes," she said. "I am very sorry for your loss. Sir, how can I be of assistance?"

"I was wondering if we could meet at the accident site so I can ask a few questions."

"When would you like to do this?"

"When could you be available?"

"Well, I'm off duty today, but I would be willing to meet there about three p.m. Would that work for you?"

"That'll work fine."

She said, "Do you know the intersection where this happened?"

"No, can you tell me?"

"It's at the intersection of Highway M. M. and Highway 12."

"Right. I know where that is. Thank you. I will see you at three."

"Okay." She hung up.

Ringo was leaning back in the seat with his ball cap pulled low over his eyes. Jack opened the door, which startled him. Ringo said, "Well, what did he say?"

"It was a she," said Jack, "and she said we could meet her at the crash site at three p.m. today."

Ringo looked at his watch and said, "Let's eat. I'm hungry."

"All right," said Jack. "There was a diner on the main drag that I saw when we drove through town. It should be open."

Ringo nodded, and they rolled back into town and stopped in front of the diner. Jack decided to make a quick call to Terri to let her know all was okay.

Ringo nodded and walked into the diner. Jack smiled and walked over to the phone booth on the street. The wind had picked up a bit, and it was still very chilly. As he got into the booth, he picked up the receiver and looked across the road where he noticed a plain, black, four-door sedan was sitting with the engine running. The windows were tinted dark, and it was cloudy outside, but he could not help but notice a silhouette of two men sitting inside. "Spooks," he said in a low voice as he dialed Terri's number.

"Hello, Terri! Yes, it's Jack! Where are you, Terri? Are you okay?"

"Yeah, sure, why?"

"Just wanted to make sure. It's been a crazy day already. Did you hear about the accident last night?"

"No, I didn't. What accident?"

"Well, remember Donnie Roscoe? He was there with us at the bar."

"Yeah, I do remember Donnie. He was the real quiet guy that wasn't drinking too much, right? Why?"

"Well, he died in a car accident last night."

"Oh God, Jack, I am so sorry! What happened?"

"Well nothing is official right now, but the impression I am getting is they think he went off the road and hit something or someone and died. He had been drinking, so they will find alcohol in his blood, or most likely they already know that. They will probably assume he was drunk."

"Oh God, Jack."

"Ringo and I are going to meet the officer that was on the scene last night at three p.m. today to go over a few things. Ringo is in the café waiting for me right now."

"Jack, does this have anything to do with those guys in the bar last night?"

"I don't know, Terri. I will see you later. Then we can talk. Will that be okay?"

"Yeah, that will be fine. Make sure you are careful. I don't like the way things are playing out right now."

"Yeah, me neither. Something is going on, and I'm bound and determined to figure out what it is. I'll talk to you soon. Stay safe and watch your back today."

Jack hung up the phone and walked out of the telephone booth and noticed the two guys in the sedan were gone. Jack walked into the diner and saw Ringo getting friendly with the waitress. She was smiling and blushing a little; then she giggled and shook her hair from side to side and put a little extra swing in her rear as she strutted back to the kitchen. Jack looked at Ringo. "Well, looks like you make new friends easily."

"Not yet, but time will tell if we are going to be good friends."

"Cool it down there, hot rod. This is a small town, and she may have an attachment to somebody!"

Ringo laughed. "That's okay, I'll share!"

"Yeah, but is the other guy as willing to share?"

Ringo let out another laugh. Jack knew Ringo well enough to know he wasn't kidding. He really would share. "Hey, did you talk to Terri?"

"Yeah, she's all right. I will see her later tonight. Hey, when were you supposed to fly home anyway?"

"Whenever I want too."

"Oh, you don't have a job?" asked Jack.

"No."

"A family? Anything to go home too?"

"Nope."

"What the hell have you been doing since we got back to the states?" Jack knew this behavior all too well with other guys that he had known.

"I took my service money from the marines, and, you know, the money we got because we no longer exist." Cautiously he looked around to make sure no one was watching or listening.

"I saved up and bought a used trailer house on some land in North Dakota. Then I bought a used Harley and a pickup truck. I drive combines in the summer for cash to pay the taxes on the land and a little expense money. I am good for nine months out of the year."

"Don't you get lonely out there?"

"No, man. I get a visit from a barmaid in town and also one little brunette who runs a potato farm. I fix her tractors, if you know what I mean."

Jack laughed. "I think so."

"What about you, man? What have you been doing?"

"I traveled around for a while then went home and bought my grandfather's farm from the estate auction. I started traveling again, and I really haven't been home for a long time other than to check mail and pay bills. If I hadn't gotten the letter from Dave's mom, I wouldn't have known about the funeral."

"Really?" said Ringo. "They called the rest of us, I think, but since you weren't at home to answer the phone, it was pure chance you got the notice in time."

Jack said, "Yeah, I just got to the farm and picked up the mail when I saw it."

"You're not much different than I am, are you, Jack?"

"Probably not," he said.

"Did you get a job or something?"

"Well, I did go back to work for my old boss as a carpenter again."

"I never knew you were a hard hat, Jack."

"Yeah, I actually have been swinging a hammer my whole life until Uncle Sam got me." Thoughts returned to Jack that he hadn't thought about for a long time— thoughts of his youth, working with his dad and his grandpa, shaping things with their hands, making things come alive. It was a time he missed and a time he hoped to get back too soon.

Pulling him from his little world, Ringo said, "Let's order, man. Here she comes!"

The waitress sauntered up with a big smile and her blouse unbuttoned a little more and leaned toward Ringo. She looked him in the eye. "Are you inviting me over after I get off work?"

Ringo smiled and said, "You are always welcome!" She winked at him then took their orders, and they had a few laughs as she walked away to put their orders in. Ringo was eating it up, more than the food that would arrive soon. They ate their lunch, and Jack picked up the tab and went to the counter to pay for it. Ringo was writing his room number on the waitress's arm. As they walked out of the diner, Jack looked across the street.

They both noticed the black, four-door sedan again. Jack said, "I see our spooks are back."

"Yeah," said Ringo, "I noticed them when we arrived, but they drove away when you walked over to the phone booth. I figured they did the ol' 'around-the-block' routine as we walked in."

"Yeah," said Jack as they arrived at the car. "Did you leave the car unlocked?"

"No, why?"

"'Cause it's unlocked now."

"Oh, man," said Ringo, and he dropped down on his knees to look under the car. "She's clean underneath. Let's check under the hood." Ringo popped the hood and looked. "It's okay. Nothing was tampered with. We better check the trunk."

Ringo took the key and opened the trunk, and his suitcase was ripped all to hell, and the trunk liner had been ripped out.

"What are these assholes looking for?" said Ringo.

"I don't know. I just don't know! What did you have in your bag? Anything important?" said Jack.

"Nothing, man! Just clothes and—my service revolver and some ammo!"

"Is it still there?"

Ringo dug a little bit on the side of the suitcase. "Yes, it's still here!"

"Are you missing anything?"

"No, man, why?"

"I don't know," Jack said. "Just trying to figure this out. They're obviously looking for something and think that one of us has it."

"What is happening?" Ringo said.

"Not sure, man. I am just not sure but, we are going to find out, that's for damn sure."

"Come on, Ringo, we better head to the accident scene. It's almost three p.m."

Truth or Dare

They got into the car and started it up. The scene of the accident wasn't far away. As Jack drove, he tried to think of all the things that had happened in the last two days—Dave's death, Donnie's accident, the car being broken into. Nothing was making any sense right now. Luckily he didn't have much time to think. As they rounded the slow curve they saw an old Ford pickup parked on the shoulder.

A tall, slender blonde woman with long hair was standing next to the truck. She was wearing tight blue jeans, cowboy boots, a jean jacket, and her hair was blowing in the breeze. Jack walked up to her and said, "Sergeant Davis?"

"Yes."

Jack smiled. "Hi, I'm Jack, and this is Ringo. Thanks so much for taking the time on your day off to meet with us."

"Nice to meet you," she said as she shook their hands. "So what can I answer for you?"

"Well, can you tell me exactly where you found the car."

"Sure," she said, "But I didn't exactly find the car."

"Who did?"

"A passing motorist saw the accident and called from a pay phone at the old abandoned service station."

"Oh really? Do you have their name?" questioned Jack.

"No, the caller never identified himself. It was someone who said there was an accident with a fatality and then they hung up. We never got any more information than that."

"Was that a man or a woman caller?"

"It was a man as far as I know."

"How did this man know he was dead?"

"I presume he walked up and found him dead and then he left to use the phone to call it in."

With skepticism flowing freely, Jack looked at her and said, "Still you responded to the call and found him dead in the car?"

"No, actually the car was here. The driver's door was open and he was lying in the field over there."

Jack said, "So he was thrown from the car, I presume?"

"I assume so," she said. "I think the car hit this guardrail and he was thrown and then the car left the roadway."

"Yeah, it looks that way." Jack said, "Did you get a good look at the car before it was towed?"

"Yes, I did, and I took photos of course. You can clearly see the front end damage where the collision occurred."

Jack said, "Yeah, must have been an unusual impact for him to hit a guardrail so hard he was thrown out but not enough impact to smash the radiator in. So it is assumed the driver's door was thrown open and Donnie was thrown out without even breaking the glass or damaging the door?"

"Well, yes," she said. "It looks like that is what happened. Some other evidence could have contributed. He had alcohol in the car and we know he came from the bar in town." Questions were beginning to swirl in the air. Jack could see the confusion in the sergeant's eyes.

"Sergeant, let's say he was impaired in some way. The whole situation would still be kind of unusual. For him to be thrown out of the car without a door malfunction or any glass broken? That seems highly unlikely, don't you think?" The concern was becoming evident in the body language of the officer. Jack had questioned her authority and her understanding of the crime scene.

"Hey," she said, "who are you guys? I was told you are relatives."

"No, we're not relatives, but we were his best friends."

This information pushed her over the edge. She had had enough of them interrogating her on a case that she had investigated. She snapped. "I don't know what else I can tell you guys. It's all in my report. I filed it last night at the station. If you need more information than that, you can go check it all out there. We're done here."

She turned and walked back to her truck. Jack walked up and tapped on the glass. As she rolled down the window she continued to look straight ahead. Jack could tell she was pissed off big time.

Jack said, "Hey, I don't mean to be an asshole here, but we just lost a friend, and it seems a little unusual."

Slowly and precisely, she turned toward him and said, "Hey, it happens that way sometimes." She started the truck and said, "Excuse me, sir, but if you don't step aside, I will have to run you over. I am in a bit of a hurry. I have horses to attend to." She rolled the window back up and dropped her truck in gear. Jack jumped back a step or two as she spun a little gravel and headed down the highway.

Jack and Ringo looked at each other and Jack said, "I think we struck a nerve there."

"No joke! She has a five-hundred-pound ape on her back," said Ringo. "Maybe somebody has control of the situation, it's not her, and she can't say much."

Jack and Ringo looked around a little more at the crash site as the autumn sun started to set. They didn't see anything else that could tell them what had happened, so they got back into the car and headed toward Terri's house. Jack glanced in the rearview window and noticed they had company. "Hey, Ringo. See those spooks on our tail?"

Ringo looked into the side mirror and said, "Yeah! Who are these guys? They sure don't know how to tail somebody, do they?"

"No, they don't."

"Maybe we should find out who these guys are. Is your gun still in the trunk?"

"No way, man. I have it loaded and in my belt. How about you?"

Jack said, "I have two full-auto .45s under my jacket—loaded, and the safety is off."

Ringo yelled out, "You thinking what I'm thinking?" Jack nodded a yes as Ringo looked over at him with a grin.

"Hold on," said Ringo as he hit the brakes and turned the wheel hard. The car spun completely around, and they were heading straight at the car that had been tailing them.

He put the pedal to the metal and said, "Come on, you idiots!"

Jack said, "Okay, you chicken. Let's see if you got the balls!"

They headed down the road straight at the car, accelerating faster and faster. Ringo started flashing his headlights on and off, trying to freak them out. They got within a couple of car lengths when the sedan finally jerked off the road to the right and hit the ditch. It rolled into the mud and water and landed on its roof.

Ringo slammed on the brakes and turned the car around and pulled up to the side of the road. He flipped on the bright lights so they were glaring on the car. The tires were still spinning, and steam was coming from the engine and off the hot exhaust pipes. The two guys in suits and ties came crawling out of the windows, both of them scratched and bleeding.

Jack and Ringo jumped out and pulled out their guns, pointing them at the two guys. They were standing in the muddy water up to their ankles. Dusk was beginning to set, and it was cold enough that you can see their breath as they huffed and puffed from the excitement of what had just occurred.

Blinded by the bright headlights of Ringo's car, the suits stood fumbling for their weapons when Ringo said, "I've got the driver."

Jack said, "Good," as he has held a gun in his left hand aimed at the other guy. He then pulled out his other gun with his right hand and aimed that gun at the driver as well.

Jack said, "Don't even blink. Now drop those weapons real slow."

They obliged. Shaking their heads, they slowly dropped their weapons into the cold, muddy water.

As they stood there with guns pointed at them, they both began to shake. They were not sure if they were shaking because of the cold water they were standing in or from the experience they had just survived, it was hard to tell.

"Now get over here and stand in front of the headlights so I can see you," demanded Jack.

Slowly the two guys began to move toward Ringo's car. They staggered a bit as they walked through the ditch and up the embankment toward the car waiting for them.

As they approached, the car's light allowed for recognition. Ringo said, "Well, look at Dennis Hopper and Neil Young!"

"Let's see your badges, smart guys," said Jack.

Ringo said, "Come on, sir. Let's shoot them in the head! It's really cool when you do that. It makes a popping sound when their heads explode!"

What little color was left in their faces diminished immediately with the sound of Ringo's voice. Jack looked at Ringo and smiled. "No, not yet. They have something to tell us. Don't you, boys? Now let's see the badges. You know, your FBI badges!"

They looked completely surprised. Jack said, "You don't fool anybody."

They carefully opened their badges and held them in the air for Jack and Ringo to see.

"Now throw them up here." They both did as they were told. Jack continued to hold his guns on them while Ringo picked up their badges. "It says Smith and Wilson. Oh God! You guys should have stuck with Young and Hopper!"

"Hey, these guys are rookies, Jack!"

"No kidding," said Jack, "Who would've figured that out? Okay, you rookies, why are you guys assigned to us?"

They looked at each other and Smith said, "We don't know exactly."

Jack, with frustration mounting, said, "What kind of answer was that? You are about to be shot in the head if you jerk me around, and that's if I stay in a good mood. If I get in a bad mood I'm going to torture you all night and kill you anyway! If you tell me the truth, I may let you live."

"All right, all right" said Wilson. "We were ordered just to watch you and send daily reports into headquarters of your whereabouts and contacts."

"Who exactly are you assigned to?"

"You, sir!"

"What about the other guys? You had spooks all around the funeral yesterday."

"Yeah, we picked up on that, but as far as we know they are not FBI."

Jack walked up to Wilson and put his gun to his head, "Don't even think about lying to me, boy. My friend died last night, and it was no accident. What do you know about it? I want the truth, and I know when you're not telling me the truth."

"Nothing. We were on you all night. We staked out the hotel and watched you."

Jack said, "You tapped the phone of course."

"Of course," he said. "It's SOP!"

"Yeah," said Jack. "If you weren't covering Donnie, then who was?"

"We don't know."

"Well, who gives you your orders?" Jack put his gun up to his temple.

Shaking, he said, "Daniels, sir. A guy they call Captain Daniels!"

"Well, what is it that Mr. Daniels thinks we are doing?"

"Not sure, sir. We were told you may be a threat to national security."

"Why?" demands Jack.

"We were told you might have classified information that could be a threat to national security. That's all we know!"

Again Jack pushed the gun hard to his head and said, "Did you kill Donnie!"

"No, no! No way! We told you we were assigned to you. We don't know who the others are, I swear!" The men were visibly shaken, and a part of Jack believed that they were telling the truth.

Jack put the safety back on his guns and put them in the holsters. He looked over at Ringo, and he nodded and mumbled under his breath, "I know. Stand down."

Then Ringo said, "Come on, Jack. Can't we pop these bastards?"

"No, God damn it! I said stand down!" Jack snapped.

Ringo snapped back his gun holster. He looked at Jack and said, "Yes, sir!"

Jack faced the two men standing in the headlights, shivering. "Don't mind my friend. He can be a little unstable. You guys have a lot to learn. Try not to get yourself killed while doing it, okay? You really have no idea who you are dealing with, and you kids don't want to find out."

Just then the sheriff pulled up and got out of his car. "Anyone hurt?"

"No, I don't think so, sir," answered Smith. "These two guys just stopped to check on us."

"Well, I see," said the sheriff as he looked over at the rolled-over car upside down in the ditch.

"What happened here?"

Smith said, "Well, I took my eyes off the road, I guess."

The sheriff looked down at them and said, "Looks like you lost your guns and badges too?"

"Yeah, we dropped them in the water."

He looked at Jack and said, "Did you see the accident?"

"No, sir, sorry. We just stopped by when we saw the car rolled over in the ditch."

"Yeah, right," said the sheriff as he looked at Jack and Ringo. "You guys can go now. Thanks for stopping."

Ringo and Jack turned and walked back to their car and drove away. Looking in the mirror, Ringo said, "He didn't believe that, did he?"

"No, and I'm not so sure we should believe him either."

"Why?"

"Not sure if he was even a real sheriff!" said Jack.

"Why do you say that?"

"Come on, Ringo. The signs were there. No call for an ambulance, he didn't check the car for other passengers inside, he didn't ask too many questions, he didn't ask for our ID, and of course unless he was a complete idiot, he would have found out we were packing guns!"

"Yeah, that would have been fun," Ringo said. "If he wasn't a real sheriff, then who the hell was he?"

"I'm not sure. I don't think those rookies would know a real sheriff from their own grandmother. Anyway we have a complicated mess here, and I am not sure who we can trust."

"So who or where are we going to get answers about Donnie?"

"Not sure, Ringo, but I think they thought Donnie had or knew something. And they wanted it so bad they are willing to kill anybody for it."

They both were silent for while as they drove down the highway looking into the darkness. Then Ringo finally said, "Do you think Dave really committed suicide or did somebody take him out and make it look like suicide?"

Jack paused for a moment. This was the same thing he had thought when he received the letter in the mail. "I think something is very wrong here and these guys have been trying to find out what that something is. Do you know if Dave and Donnie got into something we didn't know about?"

"Not sure, Jack. I came home and like you I got on with life and I wanted to forget everything. I did a real good job until Dave died and now Donnie. Who got these guys and why?"

"I don't know, man, but I think we have to figure this out. Are you heading to the airport?"

"No, not until the morning. I may have a friend stopping by tonight. I plan on booking a flight out in the morning."

Jack looked at him and smiled, knowing all too well that the waitress will be serving them both up something later on tonight. "Okay, man, drop me off at Terri's parents' house. I'll call you in a couple of days. We should let this cool down and find a place to rendezvous. Too much is going on in this small, little town. I need time to think and don't want to get on anyone's bad side here."

"Okay. I'll hang tight and wait for you to call, Jack."

They stopped in front of Terri's parents' house, and the front porch light was on. Ringo had pulled up to the curb. Jack shook his hand and said, "Later, man."

"Later, Jack," Ringo said as he shook Jack's hand.

Jumping out of the car, Jack walked up to the front door and rang the doorbell. As the door opened, there was Terri, waiting for him to return. "I'm glad you came over."

No Logic for Desire

The morning sun was shining through the cracks in the curtain. Terri rolled over and put her arm around Jack as he lay face down sleeping. "Hey, big guy, wake up! Jack opened one eye and turned his head and smiled. He mumbled "morning" with a dry, scratchy throat and tried to fall back to oblivion.

"What time is your flight today?"

"Not sure," he said.

"Did you schedule a flight back?"

"Nope," he answered. "I thought with everything going on, I would take all my vacation days I have coming. I called my boss last night, and he said not to worry, that everything was under control. But eventually I will have to head back home."

She moaned and said, "Well, I guess I will just have to get my money's worth while you are still here." Then she pulled the covers off his naked body and ran her fingers across his back. She gently kissed the back of his neck and whispered in his ear, "You are going to be too tired to go back, so you will have to stay here with me."

They lay there for hours enjoying each other and resting in between the excitement when a knock came at the door.

"Terri!" Her mother yelled from the hallway. "Are you in there with Jack?"

"Oh—ah—yes, we were just talking!"

Her mom sounding a little frustrated, "Well, are you too busy talking to have breakfast?"

Terri's face turned red and let out a silent laugh. Looking at Jack, she mouthed the words, "Let's say yes and stay here."

Jack whispered in her ear, "No, let's eat. I'm hungry!"

"Okay, Mom, we will come down in a bit!"

Her mom said, "Fifteen minutes, or do you need thirty minutes?"

"Thirty, Mom!"

"Make sure everything is in place, if you know what I mean." They heard her turn and creaked down the wooden staircase.

Terri stood up and turned toward him. She untied her robe again, teasing him with her body. Then she turned away and walked to the bathroom.

"I will see you right after breakfast," she said softly.

Jack looked at her with disappointment and fell back on the bed, totally exhausted. He looked up at the ceiling and said to himself, "God, what have I gotten myself into?"

Once dressed, he went downstairs to the kitchen. He could smell the bacon, eggs, toast, and fresh coffee.

Ah, wonderful home cooking, he thought as he could hear dishes, pots, and pans rattling around in the kitchen.

"You want some coffee?" Terri's mom asked.

"Please." He leaned down and gave her a kiss on the cheek and said, "I love you."

"Jack, you know I love you too!" She turned around with a big, hot, iron frying pan and looked at him with meanest and angriest eyes he had ever seen. She raised her voice and said, "Jack, you are family to us. But if you hurt that little girl, I will be cooking your manhood in this pan. Understand me, son?"

Jack stood back and put his hands up with a frightened look and said, "I didn't actually start this!"

Her mom said, "No, I don't think you did because she has always been in love with you. She has always wanted to be with you since she was a young girl! She has never said it, but I would see it in her eyes every time you came over here with Dave. She's been in love with the image that was you and now, by the grace of God, you have come back."

Jack said, "Well you know she's only one half year younger than me. It's not like she is too young. She knows what she's doing!"

"Hey, she's still our little girl. Now her daddy is working, and he does not know she was here last night. He thought it was just you sleeping in her old room. So be a gentleman, sit down, and shut up. Keep this quiet for her daddy's sake until you decide where this is going. If you two are even going to let anyone know."

Just then Terri came down in a tight pair of blue jeans and an old, white T-shirt with no bra. Jack thought to himself, *Oh Dear God.*

"Good morning, Mama."

"You keep this quiet, you hear me, girl? And don't let your daddy see you groping Jack while he is here. Understand?"

"Mama, I'm a grown woman."

"Yes, I know that is apparent. Jack apparently knows it too, but your daddy doesn't. He still thinks of you as being six years old in pigtails and riding your pony in the backyard at your birthday party! Do you get that picture girl?"

"Yes, Mama. I know. Lighten up. You think I was out doing it in the front lawn for the neighbors to see."

"It's a small town, and we don't want this getting around, not right now anyway. Your papa is having a hard time as it is. He has lost your brother, and that's killing him. To let him think he's losing his little girl too will not go well, so at least keep it to yourself for right now."

"Okay, Mama! Just cool down."

"Now you two eat your breakfast before it gets cold!" Trying to change the subject and calm down, Mama looked at Jack, "So Jack, when do you have to go back to work? You do have a job, don't you, son?"

Jack looked at Terri then smiled and looked back at Mama again.

"Yes, ma'am! I am a journeyman carpenter!"

"Oh good," she said. "Just like your daddy, right?"

"And my grandpa."

"Well, good for you!"

As they sat there eating, Mama suddenly got a sad look on her face and softly said, "We tried so hard with Dave. We really just could not move him along, you know."

Her mood had changed from the feisty, overly protective mother to the mother wounded in the heart from the loss of a son. She looked down and shook her head. Terri looked over at Jack and saw that he also was feeling the same pain as he looked down at his eggs. The reality of the moment had grabbed him. Dave was gone, and the family was in deep pain. *It will take a long time to heal,* he thought.

Suddenly Terri's mom said with tears, "You kids eat up, there is plenty," and she quickly got up and walked out of the kitchen.

Jack started to get up very slowly, and Terri said, "No, don't. She wants to be alone, Jack."

"Are you sure, Terri?"

"Trust me on this. I know her. She has to make a quiet adjustment, just like my daddy. They have to give us the silent treatment and torture themselves without talking about it. That's how they heal. It's strange but true."

Jack suddenly did not feel so hungry and drank his coffee. Terri said, "What happened with you and Ringo yesterday?"

"What do you mean?" said Jack.

"You know what I mean. You two went to the crash site yesterday where your friend was killed, didn't you?"

Jack did not answer; he just looked down at his coffee. Then she said, "And you don't think Donnie's death was an accident, do you?"

"No, I don't," he said.

She got up and stood behind him put her arms around his neck. She leaned her face to the back of his neck and said, "I'm scared, Jack."

He reached his hands back and held her arms and said, "You're okay, Terri. I don't think anyone is after you or your family."

"I know," she said. "They would have hurt us already, wouldn't they?"

"Maybe," said Jack.

"But I am scared for you, Jack, and your friends." She held him tighter and nuzzled into his neck.

"Don't be, Terri. We know how to handle ourselves."

She said, "Like Donnie?"

Jack got pissed from the comment and stood up and started to walk out the door.

Terri said, "Jack!" He kept walking out of the kitchen.

She again said, "Jack! Don't do this. Talk to me. I am sorry."

He stopped and turned slightly but did not look at her.

"Okay," said Jack, and he stopped and looked over his shoulder. "Let's talk later."

"Oh, baby, I need to talk right now. Mom and Dad have gone into their cocoons of emotional protection. I don't want to do that. I have my heart hanging out here, Jack. Please!"

Jack turned and walked back into the kitchen. She held him and stepped on her tiptoes to kiss him on the lips. He picked her up and carried her upstairs and closed the bedroom door. He gently laid her on the bed. She looked at him and said, "My dad comes home at five o'clock, you know."

He looked at his watch. "Well it's only nine a.m.," he said with a wide grin.

Time for Answers

Tuesday morning, and the wind rattled the windows in Jack's hotel room. As he took a shower, Jack thought, *Ol' man winter is definitely here.*

Maybe I should've stayed at the Thompsons' one more night; at least their place was warm. The wind was picking up speed, and it just sounded cold. As he stepped out of the steamy bathroom and onto the cold, tile floor, he wrapped a towel around his waist and looked out across the lawn. He gazed at the peaceful, little town with its white steeple churches and picket fences around most of the yards. The town was like something out of one of the stories his mother had read to him when he was little.

He smiled as he made eye contact with the gardener who was raking the autumn leaves around the pool area of the hotel. The pool had been drained and covered for the winter. This would be a great place to live if you wanted to keep a low profile and have a slower pace to life. Living in a town like this, you would have real friends and close families. *Yes, almost like a storybook,* he thought.

Then out of the corner of his eye, he saw a black, four-door sedan sitting in the alleyway behind a house across the street. He quickly backed away from the window and tugged the curtain back together. He grabbed his jeans and pulled them on, not taking the time to dry off. Quickly he reached for his sweatshirt and slipped on his running shoes. His feet were still wet, and he knew that in just a few moments, they would begin to stink, but he didn't have time to find his socks.

He opened his leather duffel bag and pulled out his service .45, loaded one round in the chamber, and slipped the gun into the back of his pants. As he leaned back on the chair, he could feel the cold barrel against his skin. He peeked out of the curtain again and saw the sedan still parked there.

Pulling his leather jacket on, he walked to the front door and stopped. His instincts had kicked in. There could be someone waiting for him in the hallway. Deciding not to take any chances, he opened the side window of the room, crawled out, and went down the back fire stairs. He jogged his way over to the pool area. His hair was still wet and the air was cold. He could see his breath as the run had him a bit winded.

He stopped and turned and saw that the grounds-keeper, who had stopped raking, was smiling at him. He mumbled in broken English, "Oh, sneaking out from girl in room." He gave Jack a wink.

Jack just looked at him dumbfounded and said, "No, no girl in the room. I just thought I would take a shortcut."

The groundskeeper leaned over and looked up at the window Jack just came out of, "Ah, yes the woman still in shower or maybe husband come home?" He smiled and winked at Jack.

Jack shook his head and said, "No—no woman in shower and no husband home."

Deciding enough was enough, Jack turned and ran. He jumped over the railing and across the concrete. He climbed up a landscape retaining wall almost in a single bound. He was now in the back alley that came out behind the parking garage. He looked down the alley and could see the back of the sedan still sitting in the same place. They didn't seem to be aware he had left the hotel, if in fact they were watching him. He paused for a moment and thought that there was no other reason for them to be sitting outside his motel room, so they had to be watching him.

There was maybe one other person staying at the motel.

He had to find out exactly what they wanted. Jack crouched down and pulled the gun out of the back of his pants. He kept his squat as low as he could as he made his way to the back of the car. He waited a moment to see if they noticed him. Nothing happened, so he cautiously peeked up and through the back window of the car. He could make out two guys looking through their field glasses, which were trained in on the hotel's front door of the lobby. He noticed that they were dressed in leather jackets and wearing shades, which was odd, as it was a cold, cloudy day.

Jack's hands had grown cold, so he put them in his jacket pockets. As he was planning his next move, the car started, and he dropped to the pavement. The car didn't move. *Oh, they are cold,* he thought. This is warm-up time. Jack kept his face next to the warm exhaust, which was now steaming up and swirling around in the cool morning breeze.

Again he slowly got up for another peek. As he slowly inched up, he had his gun drawn even though the guys in the car were oblivious to his being at the back of the car. The guy in the passenger side was looking through the field glasses again. Jack crawled up to the driver's door and counted under his breath, "One, two, three." He jerked the driver's door open and grabbed the driver by the neck and threw him face down on the pavement in one smooth motion. He stepped on the back of his head, smashing his nose into the pavement. Jack jumped into the driver's seat and pointed his gun at the temple of the passenger, who still had the field glasses up to his eyes but was frozen in the position, too afraid to move.

Jack took his left hand and jerked the shifter into drive and punched the pedal to the floor. As the car accelerated, the tires began to spin, and Jack could feel the bump as the car ran over the driver, who was now lying unconscious on the ground. The door slammed shut from the acceleration. As he drove away, he noticed the passenger had still not moved, most likely due to the gun still pointed at his head.

They sped along the highway, and Jack yelled, "Put the field glasses down, now!"

The passenger lowered his field glasses but was still frozen looking straight ahead, and he said, "Where are you taking me?"

"What does it matter? Maybe I'll take you to the same place you took my friends. I should just kill you now!"

The guy, even though frightened, was somewhat calm, cool, and collected, and said, "You know we number more than two. Yeah, it's more than just me you're dealing with here. Let's say something more dangerous than spooks or special ops on your ass. You know like the one you just killed?"

They continued to speed down on the highway heading toward Interstate 35. The passenger moved his hand a little toward his jacket that was unzipped.

Jack said, "Don't even think about it! You saw your buddy back there. He got off easy. If you even try, I will pluck your eyes out of your head and make you eat them! Got it! Now take your gun out slow."

Jack used his elbow to power down the window. The wind was now cold and howling into the car. Papers and maps were blowing around in the back. Jack said, "Slow, very slow, or you will have gray matter all over that fancy, lambskin jacket you got on."

The guy pulled out a service .45 caliber and tossed it out the window and into the ditch. Jack said, "Now your backup piece."

The guy started to turn his head, and Jack hollered, "Don't! Just reach and toss!" The guy didn't move. Jack took aim at the calf on his left leg and pulled the trigger. He screamed as Jack slammed on the brakes, which slammed the passenger's head into the dash. Jack put the gun to his head again.

The guy was now panting in pain and bleeding. He was holding his leg with both hands. Jack kept the gun on his head and said, "The other piece, toss it out the window!"

The guy pulled up his right pants leg and pulled out a 9 mm automatic. His hand was shaking and his body trembling. Jack said, "Toss that out now!"

His hand was still shaking as he pitched it out the window into the ditch. The cold air rushed in again, and the windows started to frost. "Good boy," Jack said.

"Now if you have a blade, this is a good time to toss that out too. Got it?"

The guy shook his head yes, and, with a bloody hand, reached into his pants pocket and pulled out a stiletto. Jack pushed the gun into his head again and said, "Toss it."

He tossed it out, and it skipped across the pavement and into the ditch, and then he put both his hands on his bleeding leg. Jack, still holding the gun to his head, said, "Good."

Jack continued driving, dropping the speed down a little to sixty-five mph. "It is getting real cold in here. Do you want the window up?"

He shook his head yes.

Jack said, "Ah, but a little fresh air is healthy. Besides you're just cold because of the loss of blood."

The guy glanced at the floor, "Yeah, and too bad your nice, black carpet is blood red!" In a quivering weak voice he said, "Where are you taking me?"

"Oh, I thought we would take a drive in the country and chat some more."

Jack saw an abandoned farm road just beyond the freeway ramp and pulled off.

They traveled down a gravel road and pulled into an abandoned farmyard. He followed the old dirt road around to the back of the house, where he saw a machine shed with its door open, so he pulled into it.

Jack turned the car off and opened the driver's door while still holding the gun at the passenger's head. He took the keys out of the ignition and put them in his pocket. Once out of the car he walked around the front of the car to the passenger door all the while pointing the gun at the passenger's head.

Jack hollered, "Get out!"

The guy didn't move, so Jack grabbed him by the jacket, and in one jerk, he pulled him out and threw him on the ground. The passenger landed flat on his back. Jack kicked him in the balls as hard as he could, and the guy rolled over and screamed in pain. Jack jumped on his leg and stomped his foot into his gunshot wound.

The guy was lying there, moaning in pain, when he whispered through clenched teeth, "If you kill me, a lot more of us are on our way."

Jack said, "Yeah, let's talk about that." Jack grabbed on an old, rusted, metal bucket and sat down, still holding the gun on him. Jack took a deep breath and tried to relax.

"Okay, who are you working for?" Silence consumed the machine shed as the guy continued to lie there, moaning and bleeding. "Look, you are in a bit of trouble here! I want to know who you work for and why you guys killed my friends."

Still silence, nothing but moaning as he continued to lie there, bleeding.

"If you don't answer, I will start shooting parts of you off! And the parts I don't shoot off, I will rip off of you!"

The guy whispered, "Go ahead. Either way I'm a dead man."

Jack said, "Maybe or maybe not. Did you kill my friends?"

"No! I didn't!" he said through his clenched teeth.

"Okay then. Maybe you will live. If you didn't kill them, then who did?" The moment of silence continued, so Jack stomped on his leg directly in the wound and screamed, "Who did it!"

The guy screamed in pain and said, "It was two spooks."

"Two guys, eh? How do you know that?"

"Because we are supposed to be keeping them from finding the book!"

"What book?"

"I don't know. Some book of all the operations the CIA had in Southeast Asia!"

Jack said, "Why do they think one of us has it?" Silence again, so Jack got ready to start shooting, but asked one more time, "Why do they think one of us have it, and who or what was in it?"

"I don't know what was in it. But whatever it was, someone very high up doesn't want the public to know about it."

Jack said, "Why would they kill Donnie and Dave?"

"They figure those guys read through it."

"Why? Why would they have read through it?"

"I don't know!"

Again Jack put his foot up to stomp on his leg.

"Wait, wait!" the guy begged. "One of your guys has it!"

"Which one?"

"I don't know. We are supposed to watch all of you and keep the spooks from killing you."

"Well, you are not doing a very good job, are you?"

The guy was holding his leg and said, "Come on, man. How about a tourniquet? I'm still bleeding here."

Jack grabbed the bottom of his sweatshirt and ripped the band off. He kneeled down and tied it around his leg.

"Thanks," he said.

"Don't mention it," Jack responded. "I don't want you to die just yet anyway. So why are my friends dead if you are supposed to protect them?"

"I was not assigned to them."

"And who are you assigned to?"

"Terri Thompson!"

"What! Terri? Why? What would she have to do with it?"

"I don't know," he said.

Jack put the gun to his head again. "Who do you work for?"

"Wolf!"

"Who is this Wolf?" Jack said.

"He works for the war department."

"What's his real name? It sure the hell isn't Wolf."

"Don't know. We get coded messages via pay phones from Washington."

"Who is your commanding officer?"

"Director Stevens, FBI."

"FBI, seriously?" Jack responded.

The shock hit Jack, and he sat back on the metal bucket and relaxed his gun. "I thought you were Special Forces or Ops or something like that?"

"I was. I became special agent undercover for the FBI. I am assigned to the president's special investigation unit for the war department."

"Then who are these Black Ops working for?"

"I don't know. We thought they were rogue agents!"

"Was the guy we ran over back in town also an undercover FBI agent?"

"No!"

"What?"

"He was just an agent."

Jack said, "Just an agent! Well, he may be dead now. Do you have any ID?"

"Just a fake, undercover one."

Jack laughed and said, "Great! A government agent with a fake ID. Imagine that."

Suddenly Jack's gut took over, and he believed this guy was telling the truth. He clicked the safety back on and put the gun back in his pants.

"Come on, let's get you to a hospital. But first let's go and get what's his name."

The guy said, "Johnson, his name is Agent Johnson." Jack helped him into car and asked, "What's your real name?"

"Ronnie."

"Okay, Ronnie, I am—"

"I know who you are, sir! You are formerly known as Captain Jack Monroe, United States Marine Corps. You did three tours in Vietnam. You were decorated five times. You also were a POW for six months until you escaped and rescued your men. Then you went declassified and you technically did not exist, actually still don't, and like the rest of your formal Marine Unit, were listed as MIA again with no records available. Where or what you were nobody knew until you surfaced stateside after the war. We know you have black belts in five different martial arts. You are a trained pilot and an expert marksman and sniper." Out of breath and in pain he said, "Am I close?"

Jack said, "Well, actually, I'm just a carpenter."

Jack walked around helped him up and into the passenger seat again then got back in the car and started it up. He took off and flew down the highway. They drove back to the alley next to the hotel and pulled in. Sitting on the curb next to the building was Agent Johnson with two black eyes and rag shoved in his nose to stop the bleeding. Jack got out and the guy put his hands up and turned his head. He thought Jack was going to kill him.

Jack said, "Take it easy, Johnson. Did you get run over?"

"No, almost. The tire hit my foot a little and pulled my shoe off."

"Can you stand up?"

Agent Johnson looked at him surprised and said, "Yeah, I can stand."

Jack helped him up and into the back seat. They drove to the hospital in Ames. Jack parked the car in front of the hospital and helped both of them into the emergency room. The nurse came around the desk and asked what happened, addressing each one separately. She looked appalled and suspiciously looked at Jack for some answers. Jack looked at them both and at her and said, "Oh, I had mistaken them for burglars at my hotel."

"Oh God," she said, as she looked at Ronnie's leg, "He's been shot!"

Jack grinned. "Yeah, I feel real bad about that. But they understood it would hurt a little when they surprised me like that."

The nurse put both of them in their own wheelchair, and one at a time she rolled them into the emergency room. Jack tossed the car keys at an orderly at the desk who caught them in midair. Jack said, "Those two guys dropped their car keys."

The orderly looked at the keys in his hand and said, "Okay, I'll make sure they get them."

Jack walked out of the lobby and over to the pay phone. He needed to call Terri at work. He wasn't quite sure how he was going to explain all that had happened.

"Terri?" he said.

"Jack, where are you. I went by the room, but you weren't there."

"Yeah, I ran into a couple of guys I used to know. I need a lift; can you come and get me?"

"Sure. Where are you?"

"At the hospital."

"The hospital! Are you hurt?"

"No, no. They dropped me off here on their way out of town."

"Okay, I am on my way. Will you please tell me what's going on when I get there?"

"Thanks, Terri," was all he said before he hung up. Jack walked outside and strolled over to the newspaper machine. He picked up a loose paper that was lying on top and started to read the article about Donnie Roscoe's accident—the accident that never made sense and had just gotten more confusing. Just then Terri drove up the drive and Jack waved and got into the passenger side.

"Jack! Look at your shirt! It is all torn, and there is blood on it! What the hell happened?"

"No worries. We decided to help someone out."

She looked Jack in his eyes. "Are you sure you're all right?"

"Yeah, I'm fine. Let's just go."

As Terri drove away, Jack leaned back into the seat and felt the gun poke him in the back, so he leaned forward and pulled it out.

Terri, stunned to see Jack pull the gun out, nearly ran off the road. "Jack! What the hell are you doing? Why the hell do you have a gun?"

"Oh, nothing. I just brought this along in case we were going to do some shooting."

"Oh, well," she said, "that explains it. You're doing some shooting?"

"Only one shot."

"Really, just one shot?" She looked at him.

"Yeah, apparently it was all he needed."

"I see," she said. "Did you kill him?"

"No, I did not kill him! I didn't need to," he said.

"Oh, great, but you wounded someone, didn't you?"

"Oh, yeah, but I took him into the hospital."

"Oh, that was nice. At least you only shot one person!"

Jack grinned and said, "Yea, the other guy I ran over."

"Jack! What is going on?"

"Honestly, Terri, I don't know. But I think we should go away for a while."

"Why, Jack?"

"I don't know exactly. What I do know is that it would be best to get out of this town for a while. Can you skip out of work, just until things cool down a bit?"

"Well, I can do what I want. I just need to let my mom and dad know I will be gone."

"Okay, good idea. We will call when we get there."

"You mean leave right now?"

"Yes, right now!"

She said, "Jack, what are we running from?"

"I have to figure that out. That's why we've got to get out of here! Keep on driving and go right to Des Moines. When we get to Des Moines, we'll park your car at the bus station."

"Jack! I need go back to the house and pack and see my mom and—"

"No, Terri, no. We must leave now! We will drive to Des Moines, and I will buy you what you need there.

You can call your mom and tell her you're okay, but do not tell her where you're going."

"Jack, I'm scared! Are my folks okay?"

"Yes, I think so. They're not looking for your folks. It's okay, Terri. I know what I'm doing! Besides it's time I get some new stuff anyway. My clothes are all rags."

She said, "Jack, I just don't know if I can. Where are we going to go?"

"Let's just say that it's going to be a surprise, Terri. Trust me. Do you trust me? And you may just have fun!"

She said, "Okay. This has something to do with David and Donnie, doesn't it?"

"The less you know, Terri, the safer you will be. Just stick with me."

"I've got to be crazy. Jack, you are making me nuts!"

"I know. I have that effect on people, so just keep driving, and could you go a little faster please? Go straight to the bus station."

Terri looked at him confused, and she was pissed off. He was being so secretive, and she was frustrated because she did not know what was going on. Jack saw and sensed the turmoil of emotions going on within Terri's head. He grinned, noting that Terri was damn cute when she was confused. But he was very concerned and nervous because he also did not know what was really going on.

They kept heading southbound on Interstate 35 until they came into downtown Des Moines. Terri saw the Greyhound bus depot and pulled into the parking lot. Jack pointed over to a parking spot behind the bus repair garage lot. Terri parked the car, and they both got out. The air was still cool even though the sun was shining. Jack squinted at the sun and said, "I need to get some shades."

Terri was beside herself as to the point of all this and started in with the questions again. "Jack, is this just an adventure, or are we really in trouble?"

Jack looked back at her and said, "What's the difference? I always thought they were the same thing. Let's lock the car and take the keys so we can hide them."

Terri said, "Where are we going to hide the keys?"

"We'll find a place." They started walking toward the lobby of the bus station.

As they passed the terminal entrance, Terri said, "Aren't we going to take the bus?"

"Nope, but wait here while I run in and buy a couple of tickets to Winnipeg."

"Oh," she said, kind of in shock. "As if Winnipeg's a nice place in the winter!" She threw her hands up in the air in frustration.

Jack continued into the terminal. A little while later, he came out with two tickets in his hands. He held them up for Terri to see then tore them up and threw the pieces in a trashcan.

Jack took Terri by the arm and led her toward the buses as if they were going to get on one of them, but they just kept walking out of the terminal and down the street. They kept walking and got about ten blocks when they came upon a Catholic Church with its front doors open. Jack looked over at Terri and then led her up the stairs and into the sanctuary.

As they stood in the entry by the coatrack, Jack noticed the lost and found box.

"Terri, give me the keys."

Terri handed the keys to him and watched as he dropped them in the box.

Terri, completely confused, decided to follow along without any questions, so she just looked at him and nodded her head.

"Don't worry, Terri, they are in good hands." He looked up at the cross and said a silent prayer that they would all be okay and there would be no more killing.

Jack then led Terri out of the church. They continued walking down the street and stopped at the next corner where there was a newspaper stand. Jack pulled out a dime and dropped it into the machine and plucked out the daily paper. He tucked the paper under his arm and walked to the bus stop, and they both sat down on the bench.

Jack opened the newspaper and began to read. He took a section and handed it over to Terri. She read the headlines while Jack read through the want ads.

Jack stood up and said, "I need to find a pay phone. I'll be right back." Jack quickly left in search of a payphone.

Terri, alone, noticed how the day was deceiving. The sun was shining and it appeared to be beautiful; however, the cold had started to kick in.

Jack returned a few minutes later. "Hey, we need to find a way to the outskirts of town."

Terri said, "Why?"

"We need to pick up our transportation."

Terri said, "Really? I suppose you want to buy a different car?"

"Yep. I think we will look for a truck!"

"Oh, okay." She responded with a long pause. "Well you got me along for this ride, Jack. I don't have a clue what's going on, but I do trust you." Then she leaned over and nuzzled into his neck.

Jack gave her a reassuring hug and smiled down at her. They flagged down a local taxi with an older gentleman at the wheel. Jack leaned into the taxi and showed the driver the address on the newspaper. The driver nodded and said, "Sure, twenty bucks will get you there."

Jack handed him a twenty and whistled to Terri. Terri nodded and walked over and got in the back seat of the taxi as Jack got in the other side.

Jack took Terri's hand into his as they drove away.

Terri looked over at him and said, "Are we taking a cab to a special location?"

Jack said, "Kind of, well at least part way."

Terri leaned her head back, closed her eyes, and said, "Well, let me know when we get there."

Jack squeezed her hand, and in his worst country accent, said, "Get some shut eye, ma'am."

With her eyes closed and giggling at the poor imitation of the country accent, she slumped down into the seat and fell asleep.

Like A Vacation

After a short ride, they ended up in an old but very well-kept neighborhood on the south end of town. The trees had lost most of their leaves and the wind was still blowing so the leaves that were still hanging on would most likely be gone very soon. As they pulled up to a house, Terri woke up and looked at Jack. "Who lives here?"

"Nobody I know, but let's go meet them."

They got out of the taxi and Jack handed the driver another twenty-dollar bill and, looking directly into the driver's eyes, said, "Hey, you never saw us, okay?"

The driver nodded and winked as he watched Terri's behind as she sashayed up the driveway. Jack grinned and told him thanks. Hopefully the driver would be able to get her out of his head by the time he got back to the city.

The cab drove away, and Jack walked up behind Terri. He put his hand in her back pocket and whispered in her ear, "I think the old guy likes how your jeans fit!"

Terri blushed and elbowed him in the ribs. As they arrived at the front door, Jack reached around Terri and rang the bell. An elderly man opened the door, "Yes, can I help you folks?" he said with a smile, showing he was glad to have some company.

"Yeah, I called about the ad in the paper," Jack replied.

"Oh, yes. Yes, just a moment, it is in the garage in the back. Go ahead and walk on back. I will be right out."

They slowly walked along an old, brick driveway to the back of the house that led to a garage, which was constructed out of stone.

Terri said, "This place is awesome! Do you think he built this all himself? It's so beautiful, and it looks like it was built many years ago. Someone put a lot of love and time into this place."

Jack looked around and said, "Well, somebody sure was a craftsman, that's for sure. This place is really nice."

Jack opened a side door and peeked inside. It was a little dark and dusty, and he fumbled for a light and flipped the switch and stepped back.

"Wow!" he said. They were stunned for a moment just staring at several antique cars in mint condition.

"We are not buying one of these, are we, Jack?" Terri said with rejection in her voice.

"No, no, too obvious." He looked over and saw the motorcycle covered with a tarp, a whole lot of dust covering everything around it. He said, "I'll bet this is it." Jack went over and opened the big, wood garage door to let some light in and then pulled off the tarp. "Oh, yeah," he said.

Terri looked at him. "Well, Jack, you're kidding, aren't you? You're not getting this, are you?"

He just smiled at her.

Just then the old timer shuffled up and said, "Oh, good, I see you opened the door and got her uncovered."

Jack had some excitement in his voice and said, "Does she still run?"

"Yes. I had her in the shop early this spring—new tires, fuel lines, oil, gear case, and the brakes were done. She was fit as a fiddle. Good as the first day I rode her home in October of 1941. Boy, I will never forget that day!" He smiled at just having the memory.

"Wow," said Jack. "She's a real 1941?"

"Yep. Bought her new and she has been with me every day since except the two years I was in World War II."

Jack said, "You buy her here in town?"

"Sure did! It was the first Harley dealership in Iowa at the time. But nowadays there are a lot of them I guess."

Jack said, "Can you start her up?"

"No, I can't, son," he said with a very forlorn face. The guy knew his riding days were behind him. Then he said. "But you can! Start her up. My old leg isn't so good anymore. The shrapnel from the war has moved around in my leg over the years, and I can't give her the hard kick over anymore."

Jack said, "Okay, where's the fuel switch and the kill switch? How about the key?"

"Well, son, they didn't have keys back then. At least this one didn't."

Jack turned on the fuel and flipped the run switch and the choke on. He then jumped on the kick-start and—*boom, thump, thump, thump*—the old Harley came to life.

"It fires right up on first kick," the guy said in a loud voice. "She is a little loud though. My buddy modified the pipes a little to make her a little faster!"

Jack was grinning from ear to ear. There was nothing like a good sounding Harley.

Terri just shook her head as she watched the bike idling in the driveway and Jack's elated face.

Jack let the bike warm up a bit and cracked the throttle and then let her idle down again. She thumped a bit like only a well-tuned Harley would. He shut it off, and the guy said, "Aren't you going to run her out down the road at least?"

"No, I don't think I need to," Jack said. "I think she's right as rain, sir! How much do you have to have to be happy about the deal?"

"Well…" He paused then said, "She's an oldie, but she served me well. Martha and I rode her from coast to coast after I retired. I just can't ride her anymore, you know. Got no real reason to keep her and no one to really give her to. So how about five hundred bucks? Does that sound okay? You seem like nice kids. You can pay as you get it, if you want."

Jack smiled. Boy, it sure was nice to find someone as nice as this old guy was. Jack looked over at Terri. She was smiling, and he knew she was thinking the same as he was.

Jack reached into his sweat pants and pulled out a wad of bills. He counted out five one-hundred-dollar bills and handed them to the old guy. The old guy smiled when he put the money in his hand and then pulled out a piece of paper from his pocket. It was the title note from Harley issued from the state of Iowa in 1941. He looked at it for a moment then handed it over to Jack.

They talked some more about bikes and trips as they both signed the title. Jack folded the title up and put it in his back pocket.

Jack and Terri started to get on the bike when the old man hollered, "Wait. Don't you want the other stuff?"

Jack stopped and looked at Terri, and they both shrugged. Jack said, "Sure, what do you have?"

"Come on in the house, and I will get it for you."

They followed him into the back door where he asked them to wait for a moment.

He disappeared as he hobbled up the stairs, and they could hear him rummaging around in a closet. He came down carrying two matching leather bomber jackets, leather helmets, and goggles, all made of black lambskin with sheepskin liners.

"Wow!" Jack said. "Real air force issue, these are the real deal!"

The old guy smiled, understanding, knowing that he had made a good decision to give this to them. They would take great care of them.

"Hey, Terri, check this out." Jack looked at the old guy and said, "This is great! We can't thank you enough."

"I think the little lady will get cold. It's October in Iowa, and it does get cold riding, you know."

He handed to Jack the big green duffel bag and said, "This fits right on the back rack. I hope you're heading south where it's warm."

Jack grinned and said, "Yeah, that sounds about right. How did you know we were going south?"

"Oh, just a hunch!" he said.

Terri's eyes lit up. "South, I like that!"

"You be careful now, son." He looked at Terri and smiled. "You kids hang on tight to each other!"

Jack said, "You bet." Jack and Terri headed out and put on the gear. They jumped on the Harley and fired it up. As they rolled down the driveway, Jack looked back and saw the old timer giving them the thumbs up with the biggest smile he had ever seen. Jack nodded and saluted the old man as he shifted the bike into the second gear and headed down the street.

Terri yelled in Jack's ear, "How far are we going?"

"For now, as far as we can!"

Two-Lane Freedom

Jack and Terri were riding hard down country roads and forgotten highways from Iowa all the way into southern Missouri. It was getting late, and the sun was growing tired and dropping low. They could see their breath, as the air was getting colder. The leaves were changing to brilliant colors of yellow, gold, orange, and red.

As the sun continued to set, hiding behind the trees, Jack pulled off the highway into a gas station with two gas pumps. One read regular and the other high test. He coasted to a stop in front of the high-test pump. A young man walked out wiping grease off his hands. "Wow! Cool motorcycle! What year is it?"

Jack said, "1941," as Terri got off and ran to the restroom.

The attendant, still wiping his hands, said, "Cold night to be out on a ride, I bet."

"Yeah, it's a little cool."

"So do you want to fill her up?" the attendant asked.

"Yeah," said Jack, "but let me do it. I don't want any fuel to spill on the gas tank."

"Sure," said the kid, and he handed him the pump nozzle. "So where are you guys heading?"

The kid continued to ramble on, and Jack tuned him out as he studied the map that someone had left lying on top of the gas pump.

Jack looked up from the map and gave the kid his attention again.

"It's getting real cold up north now!"

"Yeah?" said Jack. "We're going south. Well, maybe, that is. We're just not really sure."

The attendant laughed. "Man, does that sound cool, just going wherever you want on a Harley."

"Yeah, doesn't get any better than this. Okay, it's full." Jack clicked off the pump, put the gas cap back on, and then handed the kid two bucks.

"I'll get your change." The kid turned to walk back into the station. Just then Terri walked out of the restroom. She said, "Jack, I had to pee for last two hours, and I wish you would've stopped!"

"Yeah, I know, and I need to do the same. Grab the change from the kid when he comes back out."

Jack whistled a tune as he walked to the restroom. He looked over and saw a bulletin board that read, "The Mountain Inn, a hidden secret of the Boston Mountains."

Hmmm, he thought and took a detour to the pay-phone. He reserved a room and got the directions to the inn. As he came out of the bathroom, he saw the kid checking out Terri's ass as she was bending over to put stuff in the duffel bag. Jack walked up behind him and said, "Hey, don't get any ideas there, son. She would be too rough of a ride for you anyway! In fact, she has thrown me off a few times!"

The kid turned around, and his face was beet red. "Oh, oh. I was just checking out the bike!"

Jack said, "Yeah, like hell you were! That's all right. It's good if you look. Just don't touch anything."

"Yeah, oh yeah, right."

Jack walked up to Terri and said, "You ready to motor there, motorcycle mama?"

"Oh yeah, big daddy, take me somewhere for the night, would you? I am freezing."

"Sure. We'll find something." Jack got on the bike, jumped on the starter, and kicked it over. Terri crawled on the back as Jack looked in the mirror.

The kid had his eyes still glued on Terri, and he chuckled. They pulled onto the highway, and Jack opened up the throttle, shifting hard just to hear the pipes sing. As the sun set, Terri yelled in Jack's ear, "Where the hell are we going? I am getting way too cold."

"I don't know," he said as he pulled off on a dark, winding mountain road.

"I hope you don't plan on sleeping in the woods tonight. We will freeze!"

"Well, as a matter of fact I do," Jack said as he pulled off the road down a gravel drive. On the side of the road was a poorly lit Budweiser sign in the shape of a key that had a painted arrow on it that read, "Motel and Restaurant." Jack rolled up and shut off the Harley. They both got off the bike to stretch their tired and sore muscles. Jack noticed it was much colder than he thought, as he was numb from the wind and the loud pipes.

Terri said, "I can see my breath!"

"Better to see it than not to."

They both approached the building with Jack in the lead. Jack looked and saw Terri's reflection in the window. She was blowing on her hands, trying to warm them with her breath. He laughed and held the door open for her. They stepped in and saw an old lady with a cane who was wearing granny-style reading glasses. She was slapping her hand on top of the TV. "Damn piece of crap," she complained. "I knew that American-made one was a better set." Then she slapped it again, and it started working.

Jack said, "Excuse me."

She turned toward them. "Oh, yes, sir. You folks need a room?"

Terri leaned over and whispered in his ear that she needed to use the bathroom again.

The old woman slid out the heavy registration book and asked them to sign in. Jack filled it out as Mr. and Mrs. Smith. The old lady looked at him and winked. "You'll be in room 112 down the hall."

Terri said, "Do you have any toothbrushes and toothpaste?"

"Sure, I have sales samples." She leaned down and pulled out a box of miscellaneous stuff from under the desk. She put it on the counter, and Terri began to pick through it.

"Take what you need, young lady. You folks travel very far on that motorbike?"

"Yeah," Jack said. "Far enough, I guess."

"Damn, to be young again. Well, you have a good night now. Ring the buzzer if you need something. The phone's in the hallway, back of the lobby."

"Okay, good night," they said as they walked down the hallway to their room.

"Hey, Terri, did you call your mom?"

"Yeah, back in Des Moines."

"Was she okay?"

"No. Did you do expect her to be?"

"Not really."

"She expects you to take care of me, or my daddy is going to kill you!"

Jack said, "That's kind of what I am afraid of. He might do that anyway."

Terri gave him a puzzled looked, wondering what he meant by that comment.

They found their room and decided to get cleaned up a bit. They both showered, and Jack looked out the window to check on the bike.

"Jack, we are in the middle of nowhere. No one will mess with that bike!"

"I know," he said as he crawled into bed. They lay there next to each other, listening to the quiet of the night.

"Hey, Jack, you're really trying to protect me, aren't you?"

"Yes, yes, I am!"

"Who is it that is after us, Jack, and what do they want?"

"I don't know for sure, Terri."

"Well, why would they be after us?"

"I'm not sure, but I think they think you have something they want. And it's something they don't want anyone else to have."

Terri said, "What was it that I am supposed to have?"

"A book," Jack responded.

"A book? Who would have given me this book?"

"You would have gotten it probably from Dave." She looked at him puzzled. Jack said, "Did Dave ever give you any kind of book or anything for you to keep?"

"No, not at all!"

"Are you sure, Terri?"

"Yes, I am sure! Why?"

"I think they will try to kill us to get it, and they think we have it or we know where it is."

"Do you think we are being followed right now?"

"Not now, or at least not yet anyway. They will find your car at the bus station in Des Moines and figure we used the tickets to Winnipeg. At least that is what I am hoping. Eventually they will realize we never did go to Winnipeg, so they will start backtracking trying to find where we are."

Jack continued to explain the scenario that would play out. "They will most likely be looking at all major bus stations around the country. That will throw them off a bit. They will probably also search all the bus station lockers for your car keys and the book, of course, but they will come up empty. Getting nowhere, they will check the bus stations around the country to see if we bought other tickets. Once they realize we didn't buy any tickets and we are not showing up at any of the bus stations, they will start checking the airlines and rental car companies. They also will check used car lots for a rental or a vehicle purchase."

She said, "That's why we bought the motorcycle, wasn't it?"

"Smart girl, you're catching on. It's the last thing they will think we would do, that is to buy a bike in October and ride somewhere. They'll be confused because they can't figure out where we've gone. Some of these guys will hang around Des Moines for a couple weeks hoping we will return to the car or they can find a clue as to where we went. They may figure we hitched a ride with a trucker, or jumped a freight train or hired a private plane. They will check all those areas and options as well."

Terri said, "Well, are we safe in broad daylight on a motorcycle?"

Jack smiled. "Yeah. Winter time on a motorcycle in the mountains, they won't be looking for us here."

"Where are we going to go, Jack?"

"I figure we'd take the back roads to Mexico. They will think the only other place would be probably in the back of a pickup truck going down the highway. They'll watch the major highways for sure." He rolled over and kissed her. "We've got to get some sleep, Terri. We have to get up early because we need to cross into Texas tomorrow."

She said, "But, Jack, my ass is so sore. I don't think I can ride that far."

Jack said, "We'll just have to stop, and I will have to massage it for you." Jack reached down and put his hand on her and softly rubbed.

She murmured, "Good night."

Jack rolled over and whispered, "Good night, motorcycle mama."

Terri gently slapped him, and they both fall asleep with a smile on their faces.

In the morning, Jack awoke to the sound of the shower running. He heard Terri singing the *Sound of Music*. He rolled over and looked at the alarm. "It's five a.m. Not quite this early, woman!" He pulled the covers back over his head, hoping to catch a couple more minutes of sleep.

Terri came out of the shower and jumped up and down on the bed, "Come on, Jack. Let's go get some breakfast."

"Oh, yeah," he moaned. "What are you, a chicken or something, getting up at sunrise?"

"Yes," she said, "if that means I get up with the chickens, then yes." Then she did a very bad rooster crow and jumped up and down on the bed again.

Jack snatched her towel and jerked it off and pulled on her arm so she would fall down on top of him. "How about you come back to bed and you could be my breakfast?" Then he pulled her close and kissed her.

"Jack, no." She pushed away. "I want coffee. Beside, until you take a shower and brush your teeth, you will not touch this body!" She jumped up and threw a pillow at him and grabbed her towel back out of his hand. She wiggled as she walked back into the bathroom yelling, "Get your lazy ass up! It's a beautiful morning, and I just want coffee!"

She peeked back into the bedroom again and saw Jack sitting in bed, holding his hand up to his mouth to see if he could smell his breath. She laughed as she looked in the mirror and started putting on her makeup.

Jack sat up in the bed and flipped on the TV. He clicked to a national news channel. They were doing a story about a plane crash the day before. He lay there, reading through the room service menu and not paying much attention to the news story. He was concentrating on the menu when he heard that the flight was from Des Moines, Iowa to Bismarck, North Dakota.

Jack turned the sound up as the newscaster was explaining that the plane blew up in the sky before it made it to the Bismarck Airport.

The newscaster went on and stated that no one could have survived the crash. Jack jumped up, "Ringo! Damn, I have to call Ringo. I hope that was not his plane!"

Jack quickly threw on his pants and shirt and grabbed his wallet, where he had a list of all his important phone numbers. Terri peeked out of the bathroom and said, "Where are you going, Jack?"

"To the phone," he said as he ran out of the room and down the hall. Jack put some coins into the phone and dialed Ringo's number.

After a few rings, a man's voice answered. Half asleep, he said, "Yeah?"

"Ringo!" Jack said. "Is that you?"

"Yeah! Who the hell is this?"

"It's Jack!"

"Jack, what's wrong?" He was alarmed by the excitement in Jack's voice. "Do they have you? Are you captured?"

"No, no, Ringo! I just got up and heard the news about the plane that crashed."

"What plane?"

"It was a flight to Bismarck from Des Moines."

Ringo said, "Was it North American flight 580 by chance?"

"Yeah that was it, matter of fact, yes."

"Oh great!" said Ringo. "Now my bag is gone!"

Jack said, "You were supposed to be on that flight!"

"Yeah," he said, "I checked in and checked my bag. I then went to the bar and met this cute bartender I knew from the Harvey, North Dakota, airport. We, ah, we spent a little quality time together, if you know what I mean. So then I missed my flight and took a later one to Minot and drove a rental car to my place, figuring I'd have them send my bag to me."

Jack said, "God damn, Ringo, you got lucky!"

"Boy, I'll say!" he said. "She was a wild cat in the sack, wow!"

"No, don't you get it?" Jack said. "You were supposed to be on the plane that blew up! Is she still with you by chance?" Jack asked.

In a sleepy voice, he laughed and said, "Well, yes, as a matter of fact. She just got on top of me!"

Jack laughed again, "Ringo, the plane blew up! Do you realize that?"

Jack was amazed that Ringo either did not get it or he was not the least worried about it.

"The news said they were thinking it was a fuel tank explosion, but the plane blew up in such small pieces that there was no way to know for sure. My guess is that there were explosives on board. You need to get her somewhere safe and get your ass down here."

"Hurry up, babe. We need to move along now," Jack could hear him whisper to her. Then Ringo said, "Jack, down where? Am I going where I think I am going? And what have you not told me?"

"Listen, Ringo, this line may be tapped. Broken Arrow, location Alpha. You better go now." He hung up. Jack turned around, and Terri was standing right behind him.

"Jack! What's going on now?"

"Nothing, don't worry. Let's grab breakfast and roll out of here."

Jack was quiet as he contemplated their next move, and Terri was warming her hands with the coffee cup and silently stared out the window.

As they sat in the diner, the middle-aged waitress walked up and said, "Honeymoon?"

Jack said, "Excuse me?"

She repeated, "Honeymoon? Are you folks on your honeymoon?"

"Yeah," said Jack. The waitress looked at Terri's ring finger.

Terri smiled at her and said, "Oh my! I must have misplaced my ring!"

Jack looked at Terri, smiled, and said, "Oh no! Don't worry. I had it insured, just in case. How about a temporary one out of the case in the gift shop?"

"Sure, honey, that will work until we get to a jewelry store and we can call the insurance company."

Jack laughed.

The waitress said, "Oh, don't worry. I'm sure you will find it or get it replaced."

"I hope so. It was a two- or three-caret diamond!" said Terri.

Jack's face turned red. Then the waitress said, "Oh my, such a ring for a young couple!"

"Oh, yes," Terri said. "Doctor Monroe is so good to me." She smiled. Then the waitress gave them their check. Jack paid the bill, and they walked out.

He said, "Come on, trophy wife. Let's go!"

"Wait right there, Doctor! I need to powder my nose." She headed off to the ladies' room. Jack walked over to the front desk, checked out of the hotel, and went out to the Harley. He checked the time. It was 6:30 a.m. As he looked up, he could see the sun shining through the trees across from the parking lot. A young deer, a big buck, strutted up to a tree to rub his rack. Jack thought, *Settle down there, stud. The ladies will be along shortly, and as good looking as you are, you will be able to take your pick.*

Jack turned back to his Harley and was looking though the saddlebags. Terri came out and handed him her handbag so he could load it in the pack. Jack was looking through the bag, "We need to go to a store today because I need clothes and clean underwear, and I know you do too." he said.

Terri smiled and said, "And a diamond ring."

He nodded and started the bike. Terri jumped on the back, and they slowly pulled out toward the highway. Terri leaned forward and, in a loud voice so it could be heard over the pipes, said, "Do you like kids?"

"Yeah, why?" Jack said as he headed out onto the highway.

"Good, because I may be pregnant!"

Jack yelled back, "What?"

She said, "Hi, Daddy, I'm going to stick to you like a magnet!"

"Good! Now hang on. It's going to be a long day!"

"Are we going to need a map?"

"No!"

"Where are we going besides just south?" she said.

"I don't know!"

"I thought it might be Mexico?"

"Maybe."

"Whoa! Well, what's the plan?"

"No real plan," he yelled back to her.

"Well, Jack. How much longer do we go without a direction or a plan?"

"Until we get there!" he hollered back.

She slapped him on the shoulder and yelled in his ear, "You are a nut case, but I think I am starting to fall for you!"

Laughing, Jack said, "You think! Well that's a start anyway!"

The Homecoming

Jack and Terri rode hard all the way through Arkansas until they reached Texarkana, Texas. Once they reached Texarkana they eased off a bit and slowly cruised through town and then turned down a gravel road.

Jack pulled into an old farmhouse driveway and the bike bumped along over the tree ruts and potholes. As they idled up to the house, a black lab came bounding down the road to greet them, wagging his tail and barking a friendly hello.

Jack stopped the bike and reached down to scratch the dog behind the ears. "Hey, boy, how are you? Come on, let's go."

Jack put the bike back in gear and cruised along at a slow pace up to the house. The dog running alongside of them excitedly barking and wagging his tail, clearly showing he recognized and was happy to see Jack.

Jack rolled up to the back porch and stopped next to a couple of custom-painted, older choppers. He got off and helped Terri by holding the handle bars to stabilize the bike. As soon as Terri got her feet on the ground, she reached down to scratch the dog, and as she did, he jumped up and gave her a wet kiss on the lips.

"Ooh—ah—yuk! Dog slobbers," she said and started laughing as she knelt down. "Come here, boy." The dog came up and put his head in her lap, and she scratched behind his ears. "Boy! Are you a lover boy."

Jack laughed. "His name is Hairy."

"Well, Hairy, nice to meet you." She shook his paw. "Why do they call him Hairy, Jack?"

"Well, look at your pants."

"Oh God, he's a shed monster!"

"Yup—they call him Hairy all right." Just then a pretty woman came to the door with dishwater-blonde hair. She was wearing a cotton summer dress. There was a little girl standing beside her holding her hand. Terri noticed that she was very, very, pregnant. She said, "Can I help you folks?"

Jack turned around and smiled. Her jaw dropped. "Jack! Oh my God, Jack! Is it really you?" She rushed up to him with open arms they hugged each other tight, and she kissed him on the cheek. When suddenly Terri went, "Ah—um—mm."

Jack looked at her. "Oh, sorry. This is Terri."

She smiled and said, "Terri, it is so nice to meet you. I'm Becky," and shook her hand.

"Oh, I bet this is Jennifer," Jack said.

Then Terri knelt down to shake her hand and said, "Hi, Jennifer. I am Terri, how are you?"

She said, "I am this many," and held up three fingers. Terri laughed and then Jennifer put her hand on her mom's belly and said, "My mom is having a baby!"

"Oh, I see. Are you going to have a brother or a sister?"

"I want a sister so she can play house."

Terri laughed and said, "Yeah, I know that's good." She whispered, "I had a brother, and he never wanted to play with dolls."

Jennifer giggled; then Becky said, "Come on in, guys. I have coffee and fresh pie. You must be tired from riding on a hog."

Terri said, "Yeah, my butt is still vibrating!"

Jack said, "It always does that."

She slapped him on the shoulder and said, "Don't be rude!"

Becky said, "I don't ever mind. Yep, he's been that way since we were youngins!"

Terri looked at Jack puzzled. Then Jack said, "She's my cousin."

"Oh," said Terri, "I get it!"

Then Jack said, "Where is Roscoe?"

Becky rolled her eyes. "He is in Dallas buying custom bike parts and whatever else he can get his hands on. Lord knows we got to have more of them. I can't have a new rug or dishes, but by God, he's got to have a bad ass hog to show off all year!"

Jack laughed.

Becky looked out the window as she poured them all a cup of coffee. "Jack, that is a nice '41 you got there! Them pan heads are bad ass, aren't they?"

Jack looked at her and then at Terri, who looked confused. "Oh, Becky's dad owns the Harley dealership in Little Rock for, what, about forty years now?"

Becky said, "Yeah, sounds about right. Roscoe worked with us until Jack talked him into enlisting in the marines so they could go see the world!"

Terri's eyes lit up and said, "Jack, was he in your unit?"

Jack said, "Yes, he was."

Terri smiled and looked at Becky, who was rubbing her stomach, and said, "Well, it looked like he made it back to you okay." She smiled. "When are you due?"

"The doc said three weeks maybe. Could be more."

Terri said, "Oh, that's wonderful!"

Jack said, "What time do you expect Roscoe back?"

"Not until midnight or so."

"Really," said Jack, "It's not that far to Dallas, is it?"

"No, but he has to stop and drop off some stuff he made. Then pick up this other stuff and then load it in the truck. Then they always," and she paused for a moment and put her hands over Jennifer's ears and in a whispered voice said, "They always stop at this Go-Go Bar. It's kind of standard operating procedure, if you know what I mean?" Then she let her hands off Jennifer's ears.

Terri grinned and looked at Jack.

"Hey. You're going to stay around here tonight aren't you? We have an extra room."

Jack said, "Well, we didn't intend to come by for a free room."

"Yeah I know," said Becky, "but this way you can see Roscoe! He will be pissed off if you rolled through and didn't at least have a beer with him!"

Jack said, "Yeah, I guess we can stay. We can get back on the road again first thing in the morning."

"Oh," she said. "Where are you guys heading?"

"We are just roaming right now!"

Then Terri said, "We still have no idea where the hell we're going, do we Jack?"

"Oh," said Becky, "kind of a fancy free vacation?"

"Yeah kind of," said Jack.

"Well do you like fried chicken? I will make a batch for supper and all the fixins too."

"Great!" said Jack. "You make awesome chicken!"

Terri said, "May I help?"

"No, I got it."

"No, I insist. I would love to help."

"Well all right."

Jack said, "Hey, what about me and Jennifer? Can we help?"

"Why don't you to go out in the yard and see the horses, goats, and maybe feed the chickens? Jennifer would love it if you would put her on your shoulders, Jack, and walk around all the animals."

"You got it. Come on, Jen." He hoisted her up on his shoulders as they went out the back door.

Terri was looking out the window and watched as Jack and Jen walked up to the goat pen. Jack lifted Jen off his shoulders and gently put her down, and they began to play with a baby goat.

Becky was preparing chicken, and Terri said, "So, I take it that you and Jack have been close ever since you were young?"

"Oh yeah, he's like my brother. I used to take a lot of time off in the summer, and we would drive up to Springfield on his Harley. My dad would drop me off at Grandpa's farm. Jack was usually there working. He really spent most of his life there on Grandpa's farm. He was hardly ever home with his parents."

"Really? Why would he not spend much time with his parents?"

"Well, his brothers and sisters were older, and they were kind of mean to him when he was little so he just said screw it. Grandma and Grandpa loved him, so he decided to just stay there and his mom and dad basically let our grandparents raise him. He was there a lot of the time, and when he turned fourteen, he lived there permanently and worked for Grandpa."

"Wow, I had no idea. I guess there are many things I still don't know about him," said Terri.

"Hey, let's put this food in the oven and set the table for dinner."

"Okay, sounds good," said Terri. As they were cleaning up the kitchen, Terri said, "So how did you meet Roscoe?"

"Oh, he was a combine driver from Houston, Texas. He came here to Texarkana when I was about fifteen and would combine my uncle's bean field. He was eighteen years old, strong, good looking, and rode a Harley. I brought him over to the shop to meet my daddy, and they kind of hit it off. He stayed and went to work for us. About a year later he went to my daddy and told him that we wanted to get married."

"Really! At sixteen! Were you pregnant?"

"No, no, I just loved him, and he loved me, and my daddy let us get married. Daddy was nervous, but once he saw how well he treated me, he gave us his blessing."

"What about your mother?"

"Oh, Mama died when I was about ten in a car accident."

"Oh, I'm sorry, Becky. I didn't know."

"Oh, don't you worry. You didn't know."

Terri said, "I know, but I still am sorry. I understand your pain."

"Oh, did you lose your mama too?"

"No, just others I loved."

Becky said, "Oh yeah. Roscoe and I talked about Dave a lot. I'm sorry. Well you should go get those two. I think the chicken is ready."

Terri said, "Yeah, it smells good!" She opened the back door and hollered out to Jack and Jen. Terri walked out to meet them.

Jack said, "Oh, I didn't think you'd eat. You are as little as a bug! I'm going to call you Jen Bug!" Then Jack said, "Come on, Jen Bug, let's race."

Jack took one of her hands, and Terri took the other. They raised her up off her feet and ran her to the back door. Becky said, "Both of you need to wash up after handling those animals." They both ran for the sink.

Jack said, "Hey, Jen Bug, how about I hold you up and you can wash your feet too!" She giggled as Jack and Terri tickled her feet. They all sat down at the table, and Jack did the blessing and ended it with, "Let's have a wonderful meal."

As they ate they made small talk about life, kids, friends, and family. Once dinner was over, Jack said, "Becky, you did the cooking, so Jen Bug and I will do the dishes, okay?"

"Sure, Jack, you go ahead," said Becky. "Terri and I will have a cup of tea in the front room." After the dishes were done, Jack and Jen joined them, and Jack started a fire. He settled down in a chair and lifted Jen Bug on his lap and read her a story. A few pages into the book, she fell fast asleep on his lap. Terri looked at the two of them and was amazed at how gentle he as with her.

Becky whispered, "Come on, Jack. Let's put this little girl to bed." They tucked her in and walked back to the front room and sat down with Terri and talked a little more.

Then Becky said, "I need to turn in. Goodnight, guys. If you need anything, just knock. Roscoe will roll in late, so don't let him scare the hell out of you as he comes stomping through the door with his size-fourteen boots."

Jack laughed. "Don't worry. We won't."

Terri said, "Can I use the phone? I need to check in with my mom and dad."

"Yeah, go ahead and help yourself."

"I will pay for the call."

"It's okay. Don't worry. Roscoe has a business line for his bikes and all that stuff, so no need to worry about it. Okay, good night." Becky headed off to bed.

Jack and Terri also headed off to their bedroom. Terri got in the shower while Jack was on the bed reading a bike magazine that he found on the nightstand.

Terri came out of the shower and walked over to Jack and said, "Why didn't you say anything about Dave or Donnie? Didn't she know them?"

"Yeah, she has met them, Terri, but I need to wait and tell let Roscoe all the details first. You saw her condition. I don't want to upset her right now."

Terri said, "Are you going to wait up for Roscoe tonight or talk to him in the morning?"

"I'll try to talk him tonight if I can. It would be best if I didn't wait until morning with this."

Terri walked over to Jack and sat on the edge of the bed and began to rub lotion on her legs. Jack reached under her towel, and she said, "Go take a shower! You smell like farm animals and bike exhaust!" He laughed, got up, and went in for a shower. The water was hot and steamed the room.

As Jack was lost in thought, Terri came in. She said, "Jack, how many guys in your unit came home?"

"Seven."

"Oh God, only seven!"

"Yeah, now that Dave and Donnie are gone, there are only five of us. You met them at the funeral and the pub."

"Were you all taken from the marines and trained in this special unit?"

"Yeah, Terri, all of us were," he said. "We all became Ragged Eagles."

"Jack, I am still afraid. How do you know if we're okay? Aren't we in danger here? Who is after us?"

"Don't worry, Terri. I think they are still trying to follow us, but we will always be one step ahead of them." Jack tried to keep his voice steady, as even he wasn't sure of the answers he was giving.

"But what is this all about, Jack, really? Can this really be about a book? Killing over a document about a war that is over, it just doesn't make sense to me."

"Terri, there is more to the Vietnam War than people will ever know, and I suspect whatever this book is would expose some very corrupt and dangerous people. Let's hush up now. We don't need Becky and Jennifer hearing us."

Terri was disappointed and frustrated as she wanted to understand, but trusting Jack, she finally conceded. "Fine. I'm going to bed." She went into the bedroom and crawled into bed. The bed felt heavenly compared to the hard Harley seat, so she eased into the mattress and curled up and fell fast asleep.

Jack finished his shower and walked into the bedroom. Terri was fast asleep, so he slipped into bed. He curled up behind her, slipping his arms around her, and kissed her neck.

A little later, Jack heard a truck roll up the road and across the gravel. Slowly he rolled over and checked on Terri, who was sound asleep. He quietly got dressed, slipped on his boots, and walked outside.

Terri woke up to the sound of Jack closing the bedroom door. She got up and looked out the window. She saw Jack walking up to the truck. Jack and Roscoe hugged each other. Roscoe's voice was a little loud, so Terri could hear their conversation.

Terri heard Jack tell him that they needed to talk. The conversation then moved to hushed tones and she was only able to understand some words. Then she heard Roscoe's voice rise when he said, "Broken Arrow!"

Terri continued watching out the window and saw Jack and Roscoe walk across the yard and go into the machine shed and turn the lights on. Since she could no longer hear or see them, she went back to bed. She looked up at the moonlight coming through the window and closed her eyes and whispered to herself, "What exactly is Broken Arrow?"

After several hours, Jack and Roscoe came back into the house. Terri heard Jack whisper, "You know the location?"

Roscoe replied, "Yeah, it's what we always talked about."

She then heard Roscoe go into his bedroom, and Jack came into their room. He slid into bed with Terri, and she pretended she was still sleeping. She rolled over and put her hand under the pillow. She could feel Jack's hand, and in it he was holding a gun! Terri was now terrified and a silent tear of fear rolled down her cheek. She felt cold and pulled the covers around her neck and tried to get some sleep.

Let's Ride Like the Wind

It was early, about 5:00 a.m., and still dark, when Terri awoke. She looked over and saw that Jack was still sleeping. She could hear Jennifer crying outside. Alarmed, she got up and ran out the back door and over to Becky, who was holding Jennifer and climbing into the truck. She noticed that Becky was crying and Roscoe had already loaded one of his choppers in the back of the truck and was loading their suitcases into the back seat.

Terri, bewildered, looked at Becky. "Is the baby coming?" Becky shook her head no and held out her hand to Terri. Becky told Jen Bug to say bye bye and in nervous voice said, "We will see you later, Terri."

Confused, Terri let go of her hand and backed away from the truck. Roscoe gave Terri a wave and headed out of the driveway. Terri noticed that it was cool outside and the skies were calm. Terri could hear Hairy the dog barking from the back of the truck. She turned from the confusing sight and ran back into the house. "Jack, get up! They left! They left! They left!"

"It's okay, Terri. Calm down! I know they left. We planned it last night."

She raised her voice and said, "Where the hell are they going?"

"Don't worry. They are fine! We are going to meet them. What time is it?" He fumbled for his watch. "It's after five a.m. Let's get moving, Terri!"

"What do you mean, let's get going? Why did they leave so suddenly? What are we going to do about the farm animals?"

"Don't worry about farm animals. Roscoe has a neighbor who actually takes care of them every day. Now get dressed. We have to get moving!"

Jack got up and began pulling on his clothes, and Terri started filling the duffel bag. Jack and Terri both walked out to the bike, Jack carrying the duffel bag and Terri carrying all their leathers. As Jack was strapping the duffel bag to the back of the bike, he turned and said, "Put them on, Terri. It's cold this morning." She slid on the leather chaps, jacket, skullcap, and gloves, and Jack did the same. Jack handed her the goggles, and she put them on, as she knew her eyes would water from the cold. Jack continued to do the same and then looked up and saw her sitting down on the porch step.

Jack said, "Come on. We have to move!" She shook her head no. "No, I am not going!"

"What? We have no option here! Come on!"

"Not until you tell me exactly where the hell I am going and who the hell we are meeting."

Jack was expecting this. He actually had expected it much earlier. The fact that she had lasted this long surprised him. He walked over and knelt down in front of her. He held Terri's hand and looked in her eyes, "Do you trust me?"

"I think so," she said as she nodded her head yes. Jack turned his head to the side in disappointment. She said, "Okay. Yes, I do trust you. But I don't understand from what or whom we are running."

Jack pulled her to him and gave her a deep kiss. They stood up, and he put both of his hands in her back pockets. Jack slowly pulled her in and kissed her again. He released her from the kiss and whispered in her ear, "I am trying to protect you! Please listen to me, Terri! Now come on. We don't have any time to waste."

Terri nodded and kissed him again and got on the bike. Jack walked up the steps, turned off the light, and closed and locked the door.

The sun had not come up over the horizon yet, so it was still dark outside, but the stars were still bright, which allowed them to faintly see their surroundings. Jack turned and walked down the steps and jumped on the bike. He fired the bike up, and it snorted and chugged from the cold. Jack let it idle slowly and took it slowly around the back of the shop. He put the kick-stand down and then checked all the doors and locks of the shop.

Before he got back on the bike, he looked up on the road toward the trees in the distance. He could see two plain, four-door sedans speeding toward the farm. A large cloud of dust was brewing up behind the cars and was visible in the night air. Jack noticed that the headlights were off on both vehicles.

He leaned back to Terri and said, "Hold on tight and keep your head down! No matter what, do not let go!"

"Why?" she said. She had not seen the cars coming.

He pointed to the cars that were now about half a mile away. Jack waited for a moment with the bike running and the lights off. One car came right through the front yard and drove up to the front door, and the other went around to the back door. Four guys jumped out of each car with automatic assault rifles. They burst into the house and started shooting the hell out of everything. Jack and Terri could see the flash from the barrels through the darkness in the windows as each one of them fired.

One of the guys walked back outside and turned toward their direction as he could hear the Harley, but they were too secluded, so he could not see them. Jack slipped out his .45 and put an extra clip in Terri's pocket. He handed the gun to Terri and pointed at the safety, "Click it off and point it at them! If he sees us when I start moving, fire two rounds right at him!"

Just then a round hit the shop wall right next to them. Jack yelled shoot, as he cranked down hard on the throttle. Terri fired two shots in the direction of the guy and watched him jump for cover. Terri started to shake as she realized the danger they were in. Jack shouted, "Don't worry. I know this land. We are going to get out of here."

Jack hit the bike hard and drove along the fence until he saw an opening in the barbed wire. Jack effortlessly moved the bike through the opening and drove up the ditch and onto the road.

A milk truck was coming right toward them. The driver could not see them because the headlights were still off.

The road curved a little, and the milk truck headlights suddenly shined on them. The truck swerved to miss them and then ran into the ditch. Then one of the cars suddenly appeared right behind them, and Jack could hear a shot ricochet off the handlebar. He yelled back to Terri to return fire. She turned and fired two shots. Jack twisted down on the throttle hard and yelled, "God damn. We are on the run now!" as he shifted through the gears as fast as he could. The bike was in high gear and they were racing down the highway with nothing to guide them but the early-morning light. The pipes on the bike were roaring like thunder. Jack looked in the mirror, and he could see that the other car had also pulled up on the highway and was coming toward them.

Jack slowed the bike down a bit to maneuver a sharp turn in the road. The headlights of the car in the distance were behind them. He was thinking, *They are going to catch us on this highway, so we've got to get off of it.* Just then Jack saw a two-lane country road up ahead, and at the last second he pulled off. They were still traveling fast, which caused the bike to fish tail in the loose gravel.

Up ahead there was a railroad crossing sign, so Jack slowed down. He turned onto the tracks and heard Terri yelling in his ear, "What the hell are you doing! I see a train coming!" Jack looked in the mirror and saw the car pull right up behind them on the tracks. Jack gave the bike hell and twisted the throttle down hard! They were heading straight toward the train. He could hear the horn blowing but still could not see its light around the bend. Jack continued to accelerate toward the train.

He was pushing the bike faster and faster and hitting the bumps in the rail bed so hard they could feel the springs bottom out. The bike continued to fishtail almost out of control from the bumps and loose gravel on the rail bed. Jack could see that the car was getting closer and closer in the rearview mirror. Dawn was just starting to break in the morning sky, and he could hear Terri screaming, "Stop, Jack, we are going to die!"

Jack looked ahead for a point for them to get off the tracks, and just ahead, he saw another road crossing. The train was still a ways from the crossing, but Jack could see the train's headlight now. It was coming straight at them. The train engineer now saw them and started to sound his horn. The horn kept getting louder! He looked in the mirror, and the car was still right on his tail. Jack leaned the bike hard to the right and made it to the crossing and rode right between the arms, just an instant before the train would have hit them.

Terri and Jack could feel the rush of the wind and the brush of the train on their hands as it roared by.

"God damn, that was close!" But Terri never heard a word he said over her own screams and pleading for him to stop.

The train's lights were bright, and the horn was still blaring as Jack broke the bike hard and slid it around, facing the opposite way. They both looked up and saw that in front of the train the car was now sideways on the track and being pushed along by a fully loaded freight locomotive.

Jack could see the four guys trying to get out when he heard the explosion, and a huge fireball lit up the morning sky! They watched as one guy made it out but was engulfed in fire and screaming. He was running down the tracks toward them and waving his arms frantically as he burned alive. Jack took the .45 out of Terri's hand and fired a round into his head. He dropped motionless but continued to burn as he lay there. The train's wheels were squealing from the brakes locking as it tried to stop.

Terri said, "Oh God, Jack, you just shot him in the head!"

He replied, "Hey, if I am in a ball of fire, just shoot me in the head, okay?"

She looked down and said a silent prayer as she covered her nose with her glove, sickened by the smell of burning flesh. Jack started the bike again and they sped down a back road and into the town. Jack slowed again as they moved along, looking down the side streets for the other sedan.

Terri said, "What are we doing now?"

"We have another sedan after us, remember?"

"Oh yeah," she said and pulled the gun back out of Jack's coat pocket.

He said, "Hey, change the clip, would you? I don't know how many rounds we have left."

She clicked out the old clip and popped in a new one. Jack leaned back. "You have done that before, haven't you?"

"Yeah, you forget who my father and brother were."

Just then, Jack rounded the corner and saw the other sedan. He gunned the bike, running through the red light just as a bullet hit the mirror on his left.

He shouted again, "Hang on. Here we go again."

Terri squeezed him tight as he hammered on the throttle hard twisting the grip down trying to get every bit of acceleration that old Harley could give him. They headed up toward Main Street and turned left. He was looking, but he couldn't see them, so he drove through a used car lot. While he was looking into the broken mirror he suddenly saw the sedan hot on his tail. Their tires were smoking, and the car was fishtailing as it rounded the corner right behind them.

The sun was now getting a little higher in the east, and there was a morning paper truck unloading stacks of the local rag in the street. Jack saw a garage door open just in front of the truck. It was in an old brick building and looked promising for a place to hide, so he cut between traffic and the paper truck and rolled in through the open door. He shut the bike off before they even stopped rolling, and Terri jumped off and pulled the door shut behind them.

As they turned around, they noticed they were not alone. Standing in front of them were two black guys and a Mexican guy, and they could tell they had just ridden into a chop shop. Stunned for a moment, the three guys walk up to Jack. "What the hell are you doing?"

Jack pointed out the garage door window at the sedan with four white guys wearing suits driving by real slow and looking up at the building. The black guy shouted, "Cops! Cops are on your ass!"

They all grabbed their pistols and rifles and moved toward the door. They looked back at Jack, and one of the guys said, "Why are they on you, man?"

"We boosted the bike," Jack said. They looked at the bike and then at Terri and gave her a smile. Terri stepped away, and the Mexican guy said, "Ooh yea, mamacita!" He eyed her up and down, and Jack just looked at him.

"Is this a 1941?" he asked.

"Yeah," Jack said as he stood by the side of a window looking out.

"Nice, man, real nice. It's in good shape." He then looked over at Terri's ass. "Yeah, good shape!"

One of the black guys was standing next to the open door and said, "Hey, they stopped out front!"

The guys in the shop said, "You packing, hombres?"

"Yeah." Jack pulled out one of his .45s and showed him.

"Cool," he said. Then they all motioned to stand away from the windows and doors. They peeked out the window and saw two of the guys trying to look through the windows. They could tell by the expression on their faces that they made out the bike sitting inside.

Then the two guys started to walk along the side of the building. Jack held up two fingers and pointed to the side of the building they were walking along. One of the black guys walked up to peephole that the guy was looking through. He stood up and then jerked the door open with a violent force.

The guy fell forward, and he smacked him in the head with his gun. He dropped immediately to the ground. Then in one motion, he pulled him through the door and kicked him in the head. He took his weapon and checked his pockets.

At the back window of the shop, they saw another shadow trying to look through the painted glass. The Mexican could see him, so he grabbed a metal jack handle and swung it at the shadow. It smashed through the window and hit him in the head. The guy let out a moan as he dropped to the ground.

The Mexican guy opened the window all the way and reached through it. He grabbed a hold of the guy and dragged him through the broken glass. The guy landed with a thud on the workbench. He was knocked out cold. Terri and Jack looked at each other and smiled, knowing that without their help they could have ended up much differently. But their bliss was short lived as they looked out the window and saw the other two guys get out of the sedan.

Jack watched them as they walked to the side of the building. Jack peeked out the open side door and noticed that they were carrying automatic weapons. The two guys split up, and each went to opposite sides of the building. Jack pushed Terri into the small parts room with no windows and motioned for her to get down under a bench. He looked out into the shop at the other guys and signaled that two more were out there and were on each side along the building. They nodded in acknowledgment.

Jack let the guy on his side sneak through the side door. A full automatic weapon came through the opening first, and then he leaned through the door, looking into the shop. The shop was somewhat dark, so he could not see much. He walked all the way through the door and moved toward Jack, who was now standing between a wall and a coatrack. Jack grabbed the gun and in one motion pulled the clip out, and it fell to the ground before the guy could even pull the trigger. The guy turned toward Jack, ready to throw a punch, when Jack dropped down and swept his knee, taking him off his feet. He dropped hard and flat on his back. Jack kicked him in the nuts, and the guy went into shock. He was in severe pain and rolled over, moaning.

The Mexican ran at him with the jack handle, wielding it like a sword. The bad guy pulled out his .45 from his jacket, but before he could get a shot off, Jack aimed, squeezed the trigger, and shot him in the head. His brains splattered all over the floor and wall as his head exploded from the bullet.

Jack could hear Terri crying as she huddled underneath a cabinet in the room.

The last guy dove through the shop window when he heard the shots firing. They all ducked for cover while Jack took aim and put a round right through his arm just before he hit the ground. As he landed, his head hit the concrete, and he was out cold. This was the last of them.

They all got up from the floor and looked out the windows just to make sure the coast was clear.

"Looks like we got all four of them," Jack said, out of breath.

The biggest guy said, "That's some wicked stuff man! Who the heck are you, and who are these jokers? They aren't cops."

Jack said, "I'm nobody, but they think I'm somebody."

The three shop guys looked at each other. "Man! You got these mercenary dudes on you, and you don't know why?"

Jack, still out of breath, put his gun back in his pants. "They may be ex-CIA or spooks!"

The black guys said, "Say what! Who you callin' a spook?"

Jack said, "No, no. You know, spooks—rouge agents for the government."

They all looked at him puzzled.

"These guys are killers. Usually they work for corrupt politicians or foreign governments or both."

They all looked at each other again, and the Mexican guy said, "Man that's some screwed up stuff! Hey, homes, you gonna have them on your rear now! You just killed one of them and then messed up the other three real bad! What are you gonna do with them now? You can't leave them here."

Jack said, "Bring that sedan in here, would you? We will put the dead one in the trunk and tie up the other three and put them in the back seat."

The Mexican went out, got the car, and drove it into the shop. Jack closed the door behind him. They threw the body in the trunk and tied the other three guys up and set them in the back seat. One of the guys began to wake up, so Jack punched him in the face and knocked him out again. Then the one black guy said, "Hey, maybe we should call the cops. I ain't doing time for no murder I had nothing to do with! Especially since I don't even know you or these guys."

Jack looked at him and said, "I don't think that's a good idea!" He slowly looked around at all the stolen cars and bikes that were in the process of getting cut up. Jack then walked into the parts room and walked over to where Terri was hiding. He reached down under the bench and held out his hand. "Come on out, Terri."

Terri looked at him all wild eyed and shook her head no.

"Come on. It's okay. You can't stay here." He pulled her out and helped her stand up.

"Are they all dead?"

Jack said, "Not yet."

The biggest black guy looked at Jack. "Hey, whatcha going to do with these other three?"

Jack said, "Well, they had every intention of killing us, and I mean all of us." He looked around the room.

The Mexican guy said, "Hey we don't even know you, gringo!"

"Yeah, sorry, but these guys don't care! Trust me on this. I just left another sedan and four more of these clowns on the railroad track!"

Just then, they all heard the sirens as police and fire trucks raced down the road toward the railroad tracks.

They looked at each other, and the Mexican said, "Okay, man, so get these guys out of here!"

Then the big, black guy said, "Are you like an assassin or something?"

"No," Jack said, "but these guys are."

"What! Ah man, this is crazy!"

Jack said, "Is there a junkyard around here?"

"Yeah, about five miles out of town," the Mexican replied.

"Can one of you guys lead me there? I'll drive the car there and then you give me a ride back."

"Yeah, but we had better move!"

"Terri, you wait here." He looked at the two black guys and said, "Hands off, all right!"

"Hey, chill out, man. The lady is okay with us. We get it! She can wait in the break room."

Terri, still in shock, walked into the break room and plopped down on a chair. The black guy poured her a cup of coffee and handed it to her.

Jack clicked the safety back on his gun and put it in his coat pocket then hollered, "Lets go."

The Mexican jumped in an old Chevy truck and led Jack out the back way through town and out into the country. They came to an old wood gate where he stopped and got out to open it. They drove through the gate and up to an auto scrapyard where cars were crushed. They stopped in the middle of what looked like a mountain of scrapped autos. The place was quiet, and no one was around.

Jack and the Mexican got out of their vehicles, and they walked up to each other. Jack asked, "Where is the car crusher?"

The Mexican pointed and said, "It is over there by the crane."

Jack walked back to the sedan and drove it up to the crane and parked it right under the large magnet. He got out of the car and looked around again. "Okay," Jack said, "where is the operator?"

"Oh, that would be Larry. He doesn't even wake up until about ten a.m." He made a signal with his hand of tipping a booze bottle.

Jack said, "Do you know how to operate this thing?"

"Yeah, why? Are you gonna crush the car, amigo?"

"Yes, that's exactly what I am going to do."

"What about the guys in the back seat? We can't just leave them stranded here, can we?"

"What about them? Does it matter what we do with them?"

"Well, aren't you supposed to like torture them for information or something? Like they do in the movies?"

"No! They are pros, and they know that they are going to die anyway, so all they will do is lie!"

"Hey, man" he said, "that's some screwed up stuff! You are not going to crush them alive in the back seat, are you?"

Jack said, "No, man. What do think I am? Some sort of a animal?"

Then Jack pulled out his gun and walked up to the back window of the car. He leaned in and said, "Any of you guys want to talk? You know, give me information? Talk and maybe I can spare your life."

One of the them was conscious and said, "Screw you," and spat in his face.

Jack looked over at the Mexican, who was now looking afraid. Jack looked back into the car while wiping his cheek off.

He then said, "Man, you got a bad attitude!" He pulled out his gun and, *Bang!* He put a round in the guy's forehead. Jack then proceeded to shoot the other two in the head. Their bodies twitched for a moment then went still.

The Mexican guy jumped back and said, "Man, that was some wacked up stuff! You killed them!"

"Okay, enough already. Just pick the car up, would you?"

"Yeah, yeah." He jumped in the operator's cab and dropped the magnet. He lifted the sedan up and dropped it into the crusher.

He pulled the control levers back, and the sound of busting glass and screeching metal made an eerie sound until the machine came to a stop. He then raised what was left of the car out of the crusher. The whole car was now about two feet square with fluids dripping out. The fluids had a red tint, which was clearly blood. The Mexican shouted out of the operator's cab, "Now what do we do with it?"

Jack motioned to drop it in the pile with the rest of the scrap cars. He nodded and swung the crane then hit the release, and it disappeared into an ocean of scrap. He climbed out of the machine, and they both walked back to the truck and got in and started to drive back to the shop. The cab of the truck was very somber when the Mexican, in a very soft voice, said, "You're not going to kill me too, are you?"

"Why? Did you try to kill me?" Jack said.

"No, man."

"Well, then keep your mouth shut, and you have nothing to worry about."

The Mexican nodded. "You are one scary dude, man. Remind me to stay on your good side."

Jack just smiled. "Hey, this is my good side."

The Mexican looked back at Jack and grinned as they both got into the sedan and made their way back to the shop.

Let's Just Start Here

Terri and Jack got back on the Harley and kept burning up the highway until they were tired and sore. They stopped only for food and fuel as they kept running the back roads deep into Texas.

Running along a quiet street on the edge of a town, they drove between large rows of fruit trees. The sun was shining and making shadows that seemed to dance along the pavement. Terri suddenly found herself very relaxed and found herself daydreaming as the sun warmed her face.

She leaned forward and said, "Hey, Jack, the shadows are awesome from the trees. It reminds me of being a kid in my grandfather's orchard. We used to play hide and go seek and run through the trees and hide in the shadows."

Jack was silent for a moment then leaned back and said, "Terri, we all have our own shadows to hide upon, don't we?"

Just then, he shifted down and banked to an easy left turn down an old orchard road. As they slowed to a crawl and cruised along, Terri shouted into his ear, "Where are you taking me now?"

Jack leaned his head back to one side and into her ear said, "Out into the woods to have my way with you!" She slapped him on the shoulder, and he wiggled the handlebars a bit as though he was going to crash.

She yelled, "Jack!"

"Wow! You should not do that, Terri! I could get out of control." He wiggled the bike from side to side again.

She slapped him again, and each time he wiggled the bike, he laughed and she would scream for him to stop it.

He then pulled into a narrow foot trail and drove down the path. The bike could barely fit between the trees and shrubs, but Jack was well trained to navigate around rocks and logs and all types of obstacles.

She called back to him again, "Jack, where the hell are we going?"

"I don't know for sure, but it sure is fun!"

Jack stopped the bike at the end of a trail in front of a pile of rocks. He shut off the bike, and just as Terri started to talk, Jack whispered, "Quiet," and held his finger up to his mouth. He pointed at his ears, telling her to listen.

They could hear people laughing and the gentle sound of a waterfall off into the distance.

Terri slowly got off the bike as Jack put the kickstand down and eased himself off the seat. Suddenly he heard a woman coming up the trail, laughing. She walked up to them and stopped in front of the bike. She was completely naked and wet and smiled. "Hi, Jack."

Terri's face turned beet red as she looked at Jack, wondering how he could know this woman in the woods.

Jack's eyes were fixed on her as he looked at her beautiful, naked body. He was smiling when he said, "Long time no see!"

Terri looked at Jack who was just staring at the naked lady. Terri, still in shock at the sight, found a sudden jealousy had overtaken her.

She looked at the woman again and as she said, "Hi, you must be Terri," and held out her hand for Terri to shake. Terri took her hand and shook it reluctantly as she was still in a kind of daze.

"How do you know my name?"

Jack started to laugh and said, "Terri, allow me to introduce Donna."

Terri was still shaking her hand when she said, "Why are you, ah…" She looked at her naked body.

Donna said, "Naked?"

Terri nodded yes and mumbled, "Yes, naked, very naked."

"Because we are taking a bath, and it's best to do that with your clothes off!" Donna looked at both of them and said, "Come on."

Terri could see a man standing in the water. She assumed it was Red. He had a big frame and long, red hair and a bushy, full beard.

"Hey," he said as he looked over and waves at her. "Hi, Terri!"

She waved back in a confused sort of way with a still-frightened smile on her face.

Jack was standing on the beach and said, "Red, come on out of the water. We've got to talk."

"Now," he said.

"Yes, now. It's urgent, and we're wasting valuable time."

Jack and Terri turned and started back to the camp to wait for Red and Donna. When Red and Donna walked into camp, Jack motioned for Red to sit down next him. Jack proceeded to tell Red what had just happened in town and that they were being chased by guys in black sedans.

Terri, still startled from the ordeal, continued to hold on to Jack's hand. Donna noticed that Terri's knuckles were white with the tension and realized the serious situation they were in.

Red and Jack started to talk about their next move. Terri asked again, "Where is it we are really going to end up anyway?"

Red looked at Jack. "Hey, bro. You mean, she really doesn't know?"

"No, Red, she does not know. I think it's safer that way. I haven't told anybody anything because we don't know what these guys know."

Red said, "Yeah, man, I get it."

"Did you contact Gussie?" said Jack.

"Yeah, I called his shop and the guy that paints the choppers for him said Gussie is supposed to be traveling aces."

Jack said, "What happened to full house?"

"He lost all in a draw, and now he is solo."

"Oh," said Jack. "I bet he took that hard!"

"Yeah," said Red, "I heard he rides with a bottle of tequila in his lap and star gazing through the night."

"Man," said Jack. "If he is doing that, how is he going to make it to Tango Alpha Bravo at launch?"

"Don't know, man. Ain't no way to track that wild dog, that's for sure!"

"Yeah," said Jack, "let's hope for the best with him right now!"

Terri looked at Donna and whispered, "What the hell are they saying? Is this some kind of code?"

Donna whispered back, "Yeah, I never have figured it out."

Just then, Terri said, "So where is the hotel tonight?"

Red, Donna, and Jack all started laughing.

Terri said, "What's so funny?"

"This is it," said Jack.

She said, "What! I need a bed and food, not to mention a hot shower and a place to put on my makeup!"

Jack said, "Well, you just had a shower yesterday, babe, and Red and Donna brought the grub and some bed rolls for us to sleep on."

Terri said, "Bedroll! What is a bedroll? I am not a cowboy sleeping on the range, Jack!"

"Wow," he said, "you are beginning to be a tough biker, babe. Just listen to those cuss words coming out of your mouth!"

She said, "I am not sleeping outside with the bugs!"

Red and Donna cracked up laughing, and Red said, "The bugs really are not that bad around these parts, but the snakes! Holy cow! You got to watch out for them! Make sure you sleep with panties on because they have been known to crawl right in, if you know what I mean."

Jack cracked up laughing. "Oh, knock it off, Red! Terri, I will watch out for you."

"You are an SOB, Jack!" She was standing there and had hands on her hips in a pouty, little girl pose.

Jack said, "Terri, you will live through it. It's just one night!"

She said, "Are you sure?"

Mimicking her, Jack, his hands on his hips, said, "I am sure!"

They all had a good laugh; then Terri realized how stupid she had been acting and joined in their laughter. She then apologized.

Jack picked up his boots, and Terri asked him where he was going.

"I have to get the duffel bag off the bike, and I need to cover the tracks on the trail."

"Oh, okay." She looked at Donna. "Is he serious?"

Donna shook her head yes.

"Red, where did you put your bike?" Jack asked.

"It's over there in the woods behind that small rock pile."

Jack rolled the bike over to the same spot and covered it up with some tumbleweeds and sagebrush.

Terri said, "Whose land are we on anyway?"

Red said, "It's a reservation."

She said, "You mean like an American Indian reservation?"

"Yes, a reservation. Chill out, woman, you need a joint and some booze! Life is too short to worry about where you park your bones for one night."

Terri sighed and said, "Yeah, you're right. I'm sorry." She sat down on a rock and said, "I just need to relax for a while. It's been a tough day!"

Red said, "Really? Why?"

Just then Jack said, "Hey, Red, the sun is starting to set. How about we go get some firewood and cook for the ladies before it gets dark?"

"Yeah, okay." They got up and walked down the wooded trail.

Terri leaned back and stretched out, letting her hair fall back. Donna started to remove stuff out of the duffel bag and found trees to put a tarp between.

She looked over at Terri and said, "Hey, do you really understand what is going on?"

"Not really, I guess. No, I don't. Actually I am confused as hell right now. I am riding across the country with a madman on a bike and I am not sure why these people are after us."

"Terri," Donna said calmly, "Jack is not a mad man. But for him to bring the guys together—well—you know it has to be something very serious!"

Terri said, "Has Red said anything to you. I mean anything at all?"

"No, and I know not to ask about details. He will work it out. I do hear Red and the guys talk on the phone from time to time. But I have no idea what the hell they are talking about. They have their codes, as you heard when they were talking about Gussie."

Terri said, "Yeah, I picked up on some of that when they were talking about this Gussie character."

"Did you see him at the funeral?"

"Not sure," said Terri. "I was kind of in daze, and there were so many people. I don't remember most of them."

Donna said, "No, you did not meet him, or you would remember Gussie. Believe me, he is unforgettable!"

"Donna I didn't see you at the funeral either, I don't think."

"No, I couldn't go. I had to work, so Red went by himself."

Terri said, "Well you must have some vacation time now to be here?"

Donna looked at her and said, "When Jack calls Broken Arrow, it doesn't matter what you have going. Work or not, you take off and go to the location point. When Red said we had to go, that meant we had to go!"

"Donna, can you tell more about this, or do the guys even know what the hell is going on?"

"Hey, Red said not to talk about it! But I do know some things that happened in Nam. I can't say too much. It's better that way."

Terri said, "Well they need to let me know whose side they are on. I saw Jack kill some guys that were after us today!"

Donna looked at her in shock and said, "Where?"

"Back in the town. Jack made a car crash and explode up on a railroad track and then shot a guy in the head when he was trying to escape. He was on fire! I think there were four guys in the car. They all died! Then another car of four guys followed us—well, I should say chased us into town. Jack killed one of them and hauled the other three away and came back later without the car or them."

Donna said, "Who are these guys?"

"Jack said they were hired assassins, spooks, or whatever he calls them."

"Were those guys trying to kill you?"

"Well, yeah," Terri said, "they were chasing and shooting at us." The reality of it all overtook Terri, and she broke down. "Oh, Donna. I am so scared! They were trained killers, and Jack just took them out like it was a game or something."

"No, Terri, you need to understand who these guys are. They are the best of the best. They did a lot of Uncle Sam's dirty work and lived through it."

"Yeah, that was what Jack tried to tell me. But I mean he did not even seem human! He was like a machine! Cool, calm, and completely fearless. And fight! Oh my God! He moved so fast they didn't even see it coming." Terri started to cry again.

Donna walked up and gave her a hug. "It's okay, Terri. We are with you, and our guys are the good guys, I promise. If anyone can protect you, it's Captain Jack Monroe. If you talk to the guys, they will all tell you that he was the best they had ever seen."

Terri said, "Yeah I know. I am with the right guy, but then again, if I was not with Jack, would I be in danger in the first place?"

Donna looked at her and said in a very soft voice, "Terri, listen to me. The guys don't think it's Jack they are after."

"Then who?" she said.

Donna looked around to see if anyone was coming then leaned forward and put her lips to Terri's ear. She was a little startled at her advance. Donna whispered, "I heard the phone call last night between Jack and Red. They brought you here to protect you until they can get them."

"Me? And get who? Protect who?"

"Protect you! They are after you!"

"Who is after me?" Terri began to sob again.

Donna said, "I heard them say that they think it was ex-military. Hired killers from someone in Washington looking for a book of some kind."

"But I still don't see why they would want me."

"They think your brother gave you this book or something before he died."

"Jack did ask me about some book."

"Terri, that's what it is they are after! That book!"

Terri said, "What is in this book?"

"They're not sure. It has to do with corruption and the real reason the US was in the Vietnam War. One thing Red told me was when John F. Kennedy was shot in Dallas the following Monday, he was supposed to be back in Washington to sign the executive order to withdraw all combat and peacekeeping troops out of Vietnam.

Terri looked at her. "You mean he was going to stop the war?"

"Yes," she said. "Then when Johnson was sworn in, he gave the order to escalate all combat actions in Vietnam."

"I was told it was to stop the spread of communism. That was not the reason, was it?"

Donna said, "No, Terri. It was big business. The weapons, tanks, supplies, and construction. Johnson and his business associates had a huge stake in that war escalating. Even the supply of the latex rubber trees to the pharmaceutical companies was a big part of this. Not to mention drug trafficking."

"My God," Terri said. "This is all the stuff that was in this book?"

Donna shook her head and said, "They think so. These guys saw this firsthand and didn't know one of them came back with evidence to prove it.

Somehow one of them got a hold of it and brought it back, and as you're finding out, the government or whoever these guys are will stop at nothing to get it back."

"Why would my brother have this book, if he even did, that is?" Terri asked.

Just then Red and Jack came walking up the trail. Donna put her hands to her lips to signal Terri not to talk anymore. Terri nodded and remained silent and smiled as if nothing was out of the ordinary.

Jack walked up. "Are you ladies hungry? I brought some wood to start a fire."

Terri pulled it together. "Yeah, that sounds good. How about we cook something up? I assume we have some pots and pans to cook with?"

Jack and Red started laughing again.

"Well, I guess we're going to town to get something to cook with?"

"Nope," said Jack and he held up a big ol' jackrabbit he caught.

Terri said, "Oh, issh. We are not eating a dead animal!"

Red said, "Well, would you rather we eat it alive?"

"No, but you guys just killed a bunny rabbit!"

Then Donna said, "Come on, Terri, let's go pick some fruit from the orchard down the road."

"Okay." They walked down the path to the orchard.

Jack said, "Don't be too long, ladies, because it's going to be dark, and the food will be ready."

As the girls were picking fruits and nuts, they talked about how the guys all became friends during the war and how they all bonded and are still very close for the most part.

Jack and Red made a spit and started slowly cooking the rabbit. As Terri and Donna came back up the trail, they could smell the rabbit cooking, and Donna said, "Hey, that smells pretty good."

Jack said, "It's almost ready."

Terri and Donna had filled their shirts with different fruits and nuts. Red said, "See, I told you they were fruits and nuts!"

Donna slapped him, which caused the stuff to drop to the ground. They all found a rock or a duffel bag to sit on, and they watched the sun go down. They each took a bite of the rabbit, and they all commented on how good it was, even Terri. They followed up the meal with the fruits and nuts for dessert.

The night air was getting cool, and the sun had set, so they laid out the bedrolls. They arranged them all around the rocks and up to the fire for heat.

Lying on her back and looking up at the stars, Terri said, "Where are we going tomorrow?"

Jack said, "Does it matter?"

"Well, yeah," she said. "I need to tell my folks."

Jack said, "You are just telling them you're okay and not telling them where you are, right? Like I told you?"

She was silent.

Jack said, "Terri, I told you not to tell anyone where we have been or where we are. Have you been telling them the location when you call?"

"No, I don't, but I do tell my mom everything."

Jack sat up, "Have you been calling every night?"

"Well, yeah. Every time we stop, whatever."

Red overheard them and sat up. "Terri, when did you call her last?"

"When we stopped about five miles back in the town of Dry Run."

"Did you tell her we were at Roscoe's house?" Jack said.

"Well, yeah. I tell my mom everything."

"Did you tell her where Roscoe's house was in Texas?"

"Yeah. Why?" she said.

Jack looked at Terri. "Did you tell her we were in Dry Run on the bike?"

She sat silently. Jack grabbed her by the arm. "Terri, what did you tell her exactly?"

She said, "Jack, you're hurting me. Let go of my arm!"

He loosened his grip and said, "I told you not to say anything!" He looked over at Red, who was shaking his head.

"That's how they know, Jack. They are there with her parents, and every time she calls, they know where you were last."

Jack let go of Terri and stood up. "They may just have the phone tapped, but then again it is too hard to get trace on those pay phones."

Red said, "They're not getting a phone trace. They know what she has told them, and they have her parents."

Terri said, "Oh God, Jack! Are they in the house with my parents?"

"Sounds like it, Terri, and they know everything you told them, not to mention the guys we are eliminating on the way."

"Oh God! Will they hurt my parents?"

"No, not as long as we are free and they don't get us."

"Agh," she said. "What are we going to do?"

Jack looked at Red and said, "We are not going to get caught!"

Red said, "Hey, does Gussie have the coordinates for sure?"

"Yeah. I'm sure he will be there!"

"Then you need to have Terri keep calling, but with some creative information."

"Yeah, I think you're right. We need to send them on a wild goose chase! Terri, I need you to call your folks now."

"No, Jack, they will be on us again."

"No, Terri. We are going to send them in a different direction this time."

"But what if they get a trace and track us down?"

"We are going to assume they may have done that anyway so let's throw out some bait and see if the fish bites and head toward Vegas for a while anyway."

"What am I going to tell my mom?"

"You tell her we have some exciting news! We are going to Vegas because we are getting married! We are flying in and are going to call right after we are married!"

She said, "Jack, they are not going to believe that?"

"Well, if you're really excited, they just might. So put on a good act! Their lives depend on it."

Jack looked at Red and Donna and said, "We need to ride to the phone. You guys okay?"

Red said, "Yeah, we got what we need," as he pulled an assault rifle out of his bag.

Donna said, "Will they be in town looking for you?"

"Well let's hope that is the case rather than coming up the river to this camp!"

Donna looked at Red, and he pulled out some extra magazines of ammo.

Terri and Jack got up and put on their jackets and riding gear. Red said, "Hey, Jack," and threw him another .45 auto. Jack caught it, and Red said, "Here, you are going to need these."

Jack said, "I hope not, but it's a good idea."

Then Red asked, "You need some grenades?"

Jack said, "Don't tell me—"

Red laughed and said, "Oh yea—I got 'em!"

Jack, still laughing, said, "Come on, Terri. Give us an hour, Red. If we are not back, haul the mail to the rendezvous point."

They all shook their heads in agreement. Jack fired up the old Harley, and Terri climbed on. They bounced along the trail on their way to the highway. Terri yelled in Jack's ear, "Ready."

Jack whispered to himself, "I hope so, man. I hope so."

He clicked on the headlamp switch, and the light was a steamy haze through the mist along the riverbank. Jack shifted the bike into second gear and the bike thumped and bounced down the trail. As they pulled up onto the highway, Jack saw a light up ahead in town. A local factory was running the night shift, and the large building lights illuminated the sky.

They approached the town. Terri tapped him on the shoulder and pointed to a phone booth just off the shoulder next to a streetlight.

Jack downshifted the old Harley, and the pipes made a sweet moan as they rolled to a stop. Terri got off the bike, and Jack turned off the motor. Terri pulled off her goggles and turned to Jack. "Okay, what am I supposed to say again?"

He said, "Tell them you are in Corpus Christi, Texas, and we are on our way to Vegas. Tell them we are going to get married there."

Terri smiled and leaned forward and gave him a kiss. She whispered in his ear, "I can't wait for the honeymoon!"

Jack grinned and said, "Just make the call, sweetheart."

Terri got into the phone booth and closed the door, and the lights came on. Jack got off the bike and stepped around. He saw the lights from town and heard the sound of a distant freight train roar. He could just make out a signal crossing on the side road that was now starting to flash.

He could see the train approaching, and as the headlight from the train shined across the track, he saw a silhouette of a man walking along the roadside.

He watched Terri in the phone booth. She had been talking for less than a minute when Jack walked up and gave her the signal to cut it short. She shook her head no and kept talking. Then Jack tapped on the glass and motioned for Terri to hang up. She got angry and looked at him and slammed down the receiver. She pulled open the door and yelled, "Jack! What the hell is the matter with you?"

"Terri, if you stay on too long, they will be able to trace the call."

She said, "Fine," and walked back toward the bike.

Jack said, "Well, how did your folks take the news?"

"Well, not well."

"Did they believe you?" said Jack.

"They don't believe anything I am saying."

"Why?"

"Because they think the cops are looking for you."

"Why?"

She said, "The guys you brought to the hospital in Ames."

"Yeah, what about them?" he said.

"Well, one of the guys was discharged, and he just disappeared, and the other guy died from complications, and you are wanted for questioning."

Jack said, "So this guy died from complications from a bullet in the leg?"

She said, "Yeah, that's what my mom told me."

Jack took a deep breath and said, "Terri, we are dealing with some serious stuff here!"

"What do you mean?"

Jack said, "I'm not sure yet, but trust me. We are in real deep! Come on, Terri, get on the bike."

Jack got on the bike and started it up. Terri jumped on the back, and they headed toward town.

Terri yelled into his ear, "Are we going back to camp?"

Jack shouted back, "Let's check out the town first."

"Why?"

"I want to see who may be here."

They rode into the light of the town, and Jack shut off the light and drove up a side street. He pulled the bike in between two dumpsters and parked at a loading dock just off the main street. He shut it off and held Terri's arm so she would stay behind him.

She whispered, "Jack, what are we doing now?"

Jack said, "Did you tell your mom we were heading to Corpus Christi from Dry Run?"

"Yes, I did. Why?"

"Do they think we are staying in Dry Run tonight?"

"Yes! I told her we are going to get a room here for the night. Why?"

Jack was silent. She said, "What are you thinking?"

"I'm not sure what I think. Let's watch the hotel and see if we will have our answer." Then he pointed across the street to the Dry Run hotel and parked out front was a full-size van with no windows. Jack and Terri waited in silence. They watched intensely for about forty-five minutes. Then when they saw four guys in black leather jackets, sunglasses, and black baseball caps walk out and get into the van.

Terri said, "Jack, who are these guys? Are they all from the same outfit?"

Jack kept his voice low and softly said, "It looks like it." They watched as the van started up and took off in a hurry toward the highway. Terri said, "Where are they going?"

"Vegas I hope!" Terri suddenly got very quiet. Jack was still facing forward on the bike, looking across the street at the hotel, and he said, "Terri, you did tell them we were going to get married Vegas right?"

Terri was still silent.

Jack leaned forward on the tank and put his hands on the handlebars, resting his forearms on the tank. "Terri, answer me." Terri still did not respond, so he put the kickstand down, leaned the bike over, and got off. Terri, still sitting on the bike, looked down at the ground, afraid to make eye contact with Jack. He reached over and gently set his hands on her hair and ever so slightly tipped her head back, so he could see her face. Tears were streaming down her face. This could only mean one thing—that Terri did not tell them. "Terri, where did you say we were? Tell me, damn it!"

Terri met his eyes and couldn't hold it together any longer, "Oh, Jack, I told them we are at the Orchard with Red and Donna and that we were okay."

"Why!" said Jack. "Why, Terri, why?"

Jack turned and got back on the bike and released the kickstand, when he heard Terri say in a very hushed voice, "Because they said they were going to kill my mom and dad."

Jack just shook his head in silence and fired up the bike and said, "Hang on." He took off screaming out from a loading dock with the tires smoking and the pipes roaring like the bike was as angry as he was! Terri was hanging on very tightly, and he could feel her trembling. He yelled back to her, "Take the gun out of my left pocket!"

She reached in and pulled out the gun.

"Take the safety off." She clicked off the safety.

"Now take the one out of my right pocket and release the safety."

She reached in and did the same thing. Now she had a loaded gun in each hand.

The Ghost in the Darkness

The bike sped fast down the highway. Jack had pushed the bike to its limit. The night air was cool, and the pipes roared like thunder, piercing the night's silence. Terri shouted in his ear, "Where are we going, Jack?"

"We're going back to the orchard, and I hope we get there before they do!" Just then he saw the road by an old farmhouse and turned off onto the farm field that was running along the riverbank. He turned off the headlight and slowed the bike down in order to keep the noise level down. The bike skipped and hopped over the wet, slippery rocks, splashing the water in their faces. It was dark, and they only had the moonlight to show them the way. Steam rose from the hot exhaust pipes, which made it difficult to see.

Terri struggled to hold on to the pistols as the bike bounced over the rough terrain. She leaned forward and yelled in Jack's ear, "Do you know where you're going?"

"Kind of. We just need to follow the river and hopefully we can get close enough to camp before they hear us." They continued to make their way a few more miles up the river when Jack pulled off into a little clearing between some trees. He found a big rock and parked the bike. It is very quiet except for the faint sound of water dripping off the bike onto the hot pipes. Jack whispered, "Can you hear it?"

Terri whispered back, "What?"

"The waterfall. We are close, very close. I hope they did not hear us." They got off the bike and Jack silently covered the bike with sagebrush, leaves, and branches. He turned and grabbed a hold of Terri's hand and quietly pulled her as they crept up the riverbank. A short time later, he stopped, turned, and took both pistols from Terri. They then continued following the river, using the moonlight to guide their way. They came up to the pond that Red and Donna had swum in earlier. Jack whispered, "I can see the fire is still burning. We need to keep very quiet." Very quietly they walked up to the edge of the rocks. Jack cupped his hands to his mouth and made a sound of a hawk.

A few moments later, they heard the sound of an owl. It was a calm hoot, which was Red's reply. He whispered to Terri, "He knows it's us." Jack and Terri slowly crept along the edge of the woods. They could see that Red and Donna were a short distance away from the campfire standing in some brush looking out.

As they slowly crawled up to them, Red looked at Jack and signaled that there were two men with rifles and motioned with his finger that they were around the camp.

Jack signaled back, four men in a van, and pointed across the orchard at a van barely visible in the moonlight. Jack looked at Terri to ensure she was still alert then motioned for Red to go one way and he would go the other so they could circle the camp. He then indicated that Terri and Donna should hide in the brush.

Jack could see one guy looking through the bedrolls and duffel bags while the other one was looking down the trail.

Jack watched as Red snuck up behind the guy on the trail. A quick chop to the neck knocked him out cold, and he fell facedown in the rocks. Red took his weapon and pulled him into the brush. Once the guy was safely hidden in the brush, he signaled Jack with the owl hoot again. Jack replied with the sound of a hawk. Now it was Jack's turn to take out the other guy. He slowly and methodically snuck up on the guy, who was still checking the backpack and bedrolls. He raised his pistol and rapped him on the back of his head. The guy fell forward. Jack took his weapon and gave the signal that all was okay.

Jack pulled a leather strap off his duffel bag and tied up the guy's hands and feet and made sure they were secure so he could not move or escape. He then dragged him by the feet, facedown, over the rocks and gravel to where Red was hiding. He then handed Red another strap so he could take care of his guy the same way Jack did. As Red was tying his hands, the guy started to moan as he was becoming conscious. Red kicked him in the head, and he was out cold again.

Just then they heard a scream from one of the girls. They leaped to their feet and ran toward the brush. Terri had been knocked down on the ground and Donna was screaming as she was dragged through the orchard toward the van. Red made a run for her. He was almost to her when there was a shot, which hit Red, and he dropped to the ground.

Jack's years of training kicked in, and he knew he must concentrate on the hostage. He took in the surroundings and saw that the guy dragging Donna was holding his weapon to her head. Jack, with his weapon drawn, ran up to Red to check his condition. Jack was in full alert now and was ready to fire at any time. As he approached Red, he heard Red yell, "Take the shot, Jack. Take the shot! Take it, Jack. He's going to kill her!"

Jack readied his pistol with both hands and took aim in the darkness. He hesitated for just a moment to focus as he could only see their silhouettes. He needed to ensure he was 100 percent accurate before firing. With the stealth of a trained killer, he squeezed the trigger and—*bang*—the .45 caliber cracked and echoed off the surrounding rocks. The bullet reached its target, and they both saw the guy's head explode and watched him collapse to the ground. The side of the van was splattered with blood and brain matter. Jack sprung up and ran to Donna. He knelt down to look at her and found that she was covered in blood. He said, "Oh God!"

"It's okay, Jack. I don't think it's mine." Jack let out his breath and helped Donna to her feet. Donna looked down and in a daze tried to wipe the blood and brains off her clothes. Jack left her and walked back over to the van. He pulled the keys and retrieved the guy's weapon. Jack walked back to check on Donna. He asked her if she was okay, and she shook her head yes. He told her to hold on while he went and checked on Red.

"Red, are you okay?"

"Yes," he said. "It's a clean shot. Went right through the shoulder, see. Now, Jack, help me up. I gotta go to Donna."

"She's okay, Red. Here, let me help you up."

Jack helped Red up, who immediately took off toward Donna. When he reached Donna she was still in a daze, so he gathered her close and held her tight. He gently rocked her and told her it was okay.

Red, looking around, turned to Jack, "We got one more." He then steadied Donna and handed her one of the pistols. Donna clicked off the safety, and she was back in action.

"Donna, if you're not sure who is walking up to you, then you just shoot them!"

She gave him a slight nod.

Jack crouched down to a combat crawl and headed back toward Red and Donna. He helped both of them back toward the brush and then turned to Terri. "Terri, are you sure you're all right?"

She nodded and said, "I think so." Then she proceeded to fall over unconscious. Jack pulled open her jacket and saw that she'd been cut deep near her kidney and was bleeding badly. The cut was so severe that if he didn't stop it soon, she would bleed to death. He pulled off his jacket and ripped his shirt to use it as a bandage. He pressed it against her wound, and with his other hand, he ripped his T-shirt and tied it around her to hold the makeshift bandage in place. As he finished, Terri became conscious, and he told her to put her hand on the wound and apply as much pressure as she could. She did as she was told and gave Jack a reassuring nod.

"Terri, did you see anyone else?"

"No, just one guy. He came up and grabbed me. I tried to fight him, but he cut me. He took off running when he heard the gunfire."

"Which way did he go?"

She raised her bloody finger and pointed to the creek. Jack looked up to see Red and Donna who had come over to check on her. "Hold her up and don't let her move!"

Jack drew his gun, crouched down, and took off running to the creek. When he got to the creek, he knelt down and saw the fresh mud tracks and boot prints leading down to the rocks and into the river. The water shimmered in the moonlight and in the reflection he saw some of the trees move on the other bank. He slowly crept along in the dark until he came to the edge of the water. He picked up a large stone and tossed it in the river. Suddenly a loud bang shattered the silence. Jack looked and saw the barrel flash from the gun. He lay back and pointed his gun in the direction of the flash. But before he fired he needed to be sure, so he threw another rock at the edge of the water. This time a little closer to shore. Again he heard the gunshot and saw the barrel flash. He aimed and fired a couple of rounds. He stopped and heard a thud and an agonizing moan.

Jack jumped in the water and swam to the other side. He climbed out and searched the brush.

He saw the guy lying on his back holding his face and moaning. His gun was lying on the ground next to him. Jack picked up the gun and looked at him. He stepped on his face, and the guy started screaming in pain.

Jack said, "Okay, who do you work for?"

"Screw you!" the guy said through his bloody and clenched teeth.

"Ah, tough guy, eh. One more time, and one last time…who sent you?"

"I don't know!" he said again, spitting blood out of his mouth.

Jack said, "Well you're wasting my time," and— *bang, bang*—he popped two rounds in his head. Then he said, "You didn't want to go through life with your face blown off anyway, did you? Of course not."

Jack reached down and picked up the guy's gun and threw it in the river. He checked the guy's jacket pockets for an ID, but of course he found nothing. Jack then got up and crossed the river to the other three.

He nodded to Red and bent down to Terri. "Oh Terri," he whispered as he picked her up and carried her to the van. Red and Donna were following right behind him. Donna had Red in her arms and helped him into front seat of the van. Jack went to the other side of the van lifted Terri into the back seat with the help of Donna. Jack got behind the wheel and put the keys in the ignition.

Red said, "Man, you need a shirt? You are soaking wet. Aren't you cold?"

Jack looked back and saw that Terri still had his jacket clenched in her fists. She gingerly held it up and Donna handed it to Jack. Jack slipped it on and started the van. He sped through the field, as time was of essence. Terri was holding her side and began to whimper as they bumped along on the way to the highway.

Red said, "Jack, Terri's going to need some sewing, and I might need a couple stitches myself."

Donna said, "Jack, you've got to get her to a hospital! She's losing a lot of blood!"

Jack, driving as fast as he could, said, "I know, I know!"

Red said, "Jack, if we go to a hospital, they will track us there and try to kill us."

"I know. There's a small town about two miles south of here with a clinic."

"Hey, Jack. Those clinics are not open at this time of night."

"No, but I know the lady doctor who lives next door."

He kept speeding down the highway, and Red said, "How do you know her?"

"I was there right after I got discharged from service."

"Really? What did you see a doctor for?"

Jack said, "Oh, I needed some glass cut out of my shoulder and arm."

Donna said, "Jack what happened?"

"Oh just a misunderstanding with some locals at a pool hall."

Red said, "Oh great! You're taking us back to the combat zone! How many of these guys did you mess up, Jack? And I assume they're all locals?"

"None," said Jack.

Red said, "Say what?"

Jack said, "They weren't guys!"

Red said, "You mean you got in a fight with women?"

"Yeah," said Jack. "They were dykes on bikes! About twelve of them came after me when I took their money in a pool game."

Terri said, "Stop, Jack. Don't make me laugh. It hurts, and I don't want to start bleeding again!"

Jack said, "We're almost there, Terri," as he rolled into the sleepy, little town with quiet streets. Jack parked in front of a small house next door to a clinic. He got out and ran to the front door. A porch light came on and they could see him talking to a woman in a bathrobe. They could see she was alarmed. She turned then ran down to the van with Jack.

Upon sliding the side door open the woman saw Terri holding her bloody side and Red holding his shoulder.

She said, "Come on, let's get them inside right now. Jack, I need you to carry her. Do not let her walk!" Jack picked up Terri and carried her up the sidewalk and into the house as Donna helped Red.

As Jack tenderly sat Terri down, he gave her a kiss on the forehead. "Terri, the doctor will take care of you." She nodded her head. Then he looked at Red and Donna, "I will be right back. There is something in the woods I need to take care of!"

Terri looked at Jack and said, "I'm so sorry, Jack."

He said, "Terri, no worries. We are all in this together, and we will all get out of this together." He kissed her and said, "I will be right back." Then he turned and walked out the door to the van.

They all watched Jack pull away, and then Red said, "Hey, Doc, could this take a while?"

"Yeah, why do you ask?"

"Just wondering whether or not I could have a beer?"

"No. No beer. Alcohol will thin your blood and make you bleed!"

"I thought you would say that!" Then Red picked up a syringe and a bottle from the cabinet next to him. The bottle was marked morphine, and he said, "Okay, this will do!"

The doctor said, "Let me do the lady first."

Red handed her the bottle and the needle and said, "Oh, sorry, where's my manners?"

The doctor gave Terri a shot of the morphine and then gave Red a shot. Red lay back on the chair and said, "Aw, awesome!" then passed out.

Taking Out the Trash

Early morning was just breaking as Jack was driving down the road. He was anxious to get to the doctor's to see how everyone was doing. Along with being worried about his friends he couldn't help but think to himself, *Man this isn't good. I have a stolen van with blood all over it and all over my clothes. This really does not look good.* It seemed like a very long ride to the doctor's, but he finally was there. He walked up to the front door and rang the bell. The doctor immediately opened the door and took one look at Jack and said, "Jack are you all right? You look exhausted!"

"Yeah, I'm okay. How is everyone?"

"Everyone is doing okay. Come on in and let me get you some coffee."

"So what's the status?"

"Well, they're both going to be fine. Red had the bullet pass clean right through and it didn't hit anything major. Terri is a little more serious. It looked like she was cut with a serrated knife, possibly a military style."

Jack pulled out this military knife and said, "Like this one?"

She looked at him and said, "Yes, exactly like that one. Where did you get that?"

"From the guy who stabbed her," he said.

"Oh really. This guy stabs a woman and then says, 'Oh, by the way, here's my knife?'"

"No not exactly. It took a little bit of argument, but he agreed to hand it over to me."

"Yeah, that sounds more like it." The doctor then looked at him with some concern in her eyes.

She pulled Jack's sleeve up and saw the deep wound. She put him into a chair and proceeded to prepare the wound. "Just like old times, Jack." She pulled out the needle and suture from a cabinet and started to sew him up.

Jack put his head back and said, "Great! This is just like old times."

The drugs were making him talk a little too much, so she increased the dosage so he would drift off.

After a short nap the drugs wore off, and Jack woke up groggy. "Well, Doc, what do I owe you? I need to get this group on the road."

"Oh, Jack. Forget the money, but they need to check into a hospital for a couple days until they recover."

Jack said, "No, that is out of the question. We have to keep moving!"

"Jack, you are not listening to me. Terri needs to stay in bed for a few days in order for her wound to heal. If she breaks those stitches loose, she could start to bleed again and bleed to death or get an infection. She must be stable!"

"Okay. Well, how about Red?"

"He can travel. He just needs to take it easy."

Jack said, "Yeah, right, Red take it easy."

"Well is Terri awake?"

"No, she is sleeping. I gave her some medications that will keep her down and will cause her to drift in and out of consciousness for the next twenty-four hours."

He said, "Can I see her?"

"Sure."

Then Jack turned and said, "I know I shouldn't burden you with this, but I can't check her into a hospital. Her life is at risk. Could you keep her at the house for a while?"

"Jack, who are these people that are after you?"

"Doc, I am not sure exactly, but trust me, I don't dare check her into a hospital."

"What about the authorities? Can't they help you?"

"Actually, that's the people I'm afraid of right now! I need you to keep Terri here, Doc. Can you do that for me?"

"All right. I have a nurse from the clinic that can come and stay with her during the day while I am working, and of course I will take care of her at night."

"Thank you," he said with a smile.

She smiled back at him. "May God be with you."

Jack nodded. "I hope so." He then stepped into the room and saw Terri peacefully sleeping. He leaned down and kissed her forehead. "Honey, I have to leave for a few days but the doctor is going to take care of you."

Terri's eyes fluttered opened for a brief moment and in a soft, weak voice said, "Jack, please be careful and come back to me." She squeezed his hands and then fell fast asleep again.

Jack pulled the bed sheet up against her face and gently kissed her hand.

He tucked her in again and quietly walked out of the room. He went across the hall where he could hear Red and Donna talking. He stood outside the door and said, "Red?"

"Yes, Jack?"

Red came to the door and opened it.

"Are you guys ready to travel?"

"Yeah man, but what about Terri?"

Jack looked down and said, "Doc won't let her travel for a while."

Red said, "Is she going to stay here?"

"Yeah, for a little while anyway." Red nodded.

Donna said, "Red, let me stay with her."

Red shook his head yes. "That probably would be the best thing to do right now. Wouldn't it?"

Donna walked over to Jack and gave him a big hug and said, "Promise me you will bring him back home. Promise me!"

"Yeah, Donna, I promise." Donna smiled as a silent tear escaped her eye.

Red said, "Come on, woman, you don't need to shed a tear for me. Just wait here and watch over Terri. She needs you right now."

Donna nodded yes. Red pulled out one of his .45s and two extra clips. He laid the gun and the clips on the chair next to where Donna was standing. He then grabbed her and gave her a crushing hug. They held unto each other and kissed one last time, and no words were spoken.

Red and Jack grabbed their gear and nodded to the doctor as they walked out to the van in the driveway. The doctor looked at Donna and said, "I wouldn't worry about those boys. They are some of America's finest warriors."

Donna gave her a sad smile. "I hope so. God, I hope so."

As Jack and Red drove down the road, Red was adjusted himself in the passenger seat.

Jack said, "Hey! You need to settle down there, partner, or do I need to drug you and put you in the back?"

"I am all right, Jack. I just need this damn sling off. I need to be able to move my arm."

Jack said, "Are you going to be okay with the ride?"

"Damn straight! We got our best chance to be mobile on the bikes! What did you get out of the guy you left in the woods?"

Jack said, "Not much. I killed him just like the guy I shot at the van."

Red said, "Oh! Did you at least check his pockets for info?"

"Oh yeah!"

"Well did you find anything?"

"No. But my guess was they messed up somewhere and left some info that we will find."

Red said, "What's the plan if Gussie doesn't show up?"

Jack said, "He was riding Aces. It's all up to him."

"Yeah, I guess," said Red. "Any chance that we will find the bastard?"

"Yeah," said Jack "I'm counting on it!"

"What if they kill him?" said Red.

"They won't. They'll just follow him hoping to find me and they know Terri is with me."

Red said, "How do you figure that?"

"Well, they think Terri has the book, right? They may have located everyone in the unit and have been following all of us from the day of Dave's funeral. They are not sure if any or all of us know the location of the book."

Red said, "You think they followed all of us?"

"Now, I do," Jack said. "I think they've been trying to follow us the whole way, and we just keep losing them."

Red said, "Why do they keep trying to kill us when they don't know where the book is for sure? You would think they would want to capture and torture us first for information on the book or at least get the book back?"

Jack said, "I think they figure one of us has it, and as they find each one of us, they kill us and check our stuff for the book."

Red said, "That doesn't make sense because if one of us has the book and we hide it or put it somewhere and they kill us, they won't know where it was?"

Jack said, "You have to figure that these guys are hired killers and they are not exactly what I call 'smart.' They are trigger-happy thugs who figure the book is with one of us so they will just kill us and take the book."

Red said, "You think they think it is that simple?"

Jack said, "I actually think it is just that simple. But they have no idea who we are and we both know never to underestimate your enemy."

Red nodded. "Damn straight."

Jack turned the van off the main highway and onto the farm road again. They made their way back to the orchard and into the clearing then up to the riverbank.

Jack and Red got out and checked on their bikes. Satisfied that their bikes were okay, they walked over to the brush to where they have hidden the bodies. They each grabbed two of the bodies, hoisted them over their shoulders, and then tossed them into the back of the van.

Jack walked over to the driver side and reached in and started the van. He then found a rock and wedged it on the throttle so the engine revved up.

The engine was screaming wide open when Jack shut the door and reached through the window and jerked the transmission into drive. The van took off spinning gravel as it bounced and violently crashed up and down over the beach area. It drove off the bank and dropped into the river with a silent plop.

As the van slowly sunk out of sight, Red said, "Shame to waste a good van like that."

Jack said, "Yeah, I guess."

They both turned and walked over to their bikes, and Red said, "Those four guys went for a swim, I guess."

Jack said, "Well, parts of them did."

Red looked at Jack and said, "God, Jack. You didn't eat any part of them, did you?"

Jack rolled his eyes and said, "Well, I was hungry!"

Red cracked up laughing as he pulled on his handle-bars and rolled his bike off the kickstand.

"Ouch," he moaned.

"Your shoulder? It's bad, isn't it?'"

"No, I scratched the tank on my bike!"

Jack laughed. "You'll get over it!"

Red fired up his bike and looked up in the sky and said, "Looks like it's going to rain. I can feel it in my bones. In fact my ancestors can feel it!" Jack gave him a look and Red said, "What?"

"I didn't know you were Indian. I thought you were Irish."

"Hey, I am both. I have natural skills and good luck!"

Jack laughed. "Okay, Kemosabe. Let's move on!"

Red said, "You mean Tonto!"

Jack said, "Oh yeah, I would be Kemosabe, wouldn't I!"

Sometimes You Need to Help a Stranger

The two Harleys rolled out onto the two-lane highway as the morning sun shone in the Texas blue sky. The air was just cool enough for them to put on their leather motorcycle jackets. They turned down hard on the throttles as they rode side by side. The sound of the Harley pipes rang out a song of freedom in unison as they thumped and popped down the road.

They drove up and down the Texas hills with the wind whipping through their hair. As the day progressed, the air warmed up and they were thirsty. Realizing it was time to take off their leather jackets and stretch their legs they pulled over when they saw the next beer sign.

Jack stood in the gravel parking lot and looked over at the liquor store. There sitting next to the front door was an older man perched on a plastic bucket. People walked in and out of the store not paying any attention to the old man. Jack couldn't help but notice that the man looked desperate for something.

Red walked up to him. "Hey, Jack. What do you suppose that guy is doing there?"

Jack shrugged his shoulders and put his hands out to gesture, "Who the hell knows?" Then Jack looked at Red and said, "Hey you want a cold beer?"

"Yeah, let's grab a couple of sixers and a bottle for the road."

"Okay, let's do it." They walked by the old guy and went into the liquor store.

Jack picked up two six-packs of Flagstaff beer and found a bottle of Irish whiskey and took it to the register. The register was manned by a rough-looking woman wearing an old, worn-out Harley tee shirt. Her skin was like leather, and on her right arm she had a biker tattoo. Jack noticed that she still had a hot body for a rough-looking woman.

She smiled at them. "You boys on a hard ride?"

"You could say that," said Red.

She smiled and said, "Are you going to need anything else" and gave Jack a sinister smile.

He looked at her and said, "No, no thanks I'm good!"

She looked at Red, "How about you big bear, are you good?"

He laughed and said, "Yeah actually I'm good!"

She frowned and said, "I guess I'll have to just wait for the next rider."

Jack smiled. "No worries, one will come along soon enough. Hey, what's with the guy outside?"

"Oh" she said. "That's Henry. Poor old Henry. He used to own this liquor store, but he lost it years ago."

Jack said, "Oh, did the bank take it away?"

"No, actually his wife got it when they divorced, and she sold it to the guy who owns it now. Then of course she ran off with some biker somewhere! After that Henry kind of lost his mind and couldn't even work here. So he just sits outside the door waiting for her to come back to him. I guess it's been about twenty years or more."

Jack said, "Wow that's what you call a major broken heart!"

She said, "Yeah, I guess. It's too bad because before he lost it, he was a hell of a nice guy. He used to go riding with some of the locals around here."

Jack said, "Really, where does he live?"

"Oh he has an old camper trailer in the back. The owner makes sure he has food and lets him come in the apartment in the back to wash his clothes and take a shower and stuff. The owner kind of watches out for him."

"Wow," said Jack. "Does he have any money?"

"Well, people put donations in the old can sitting next to him. Up until a few years ago, he played a pretty mean harp and used to dance a little."

Jack put his head down and shook it; then Red said, "Does he have a car?"

"No, never did. Use to ride a Harley though."

"Really?" said Red. "Does he still have it?"

"Yep. It's around back, but trust me it's not going nowhere."

They paid for the booze and told her to keep the faith. She looked at them both and smiled and said,

"You boys come back if you ever need anything. If you know what I mean."

They both smiled and walked out to their bikes. They stored the booze in the saddlebags, then Jack looked at Red, "Hey, we are making good time. How about we take a break?"

"Sure," Red replied and followed Jack over to Henry.

"Hey, Henry we hear you got a Harley?"

Henry leaned his head back and looked up. "Yeah, sure do!"

"Really? Can we see it?" Jack asked.

"Yeah, sure!" His eyes lit up.

Red held out his hand and helped ol' Henry up. The ol' man hobbled a bit at first but then straightened out his walk as he led them around the back of the store.

Red noticed his hobble and said, "Are you okay there, guy?"

"Oh, yeah," said Henry. "The shrapnel in my leg is moving around in the joint, so the old knee acts up once in a while."

"Really," said Jack. "Where did that happen?"

"Omaha Beach on D-Day!" he announced with great pride.

"Really! You were a marine, sir?"

"Yes, sir." He looked old and tired, actually too old for his age. "Sergeant Henry J. Rawlins, United States Marine Corps." He saluted them.

Jack shook his hand and said, "Captain Jack Monroe." Red held out his hand and said, "Pfc. Redman Macomb!"

Henry said, "All right. Well, I have been waiting for my relief. We've been pinned down here for last two days." His eyes started jumping around, and he started to act really strange! He bent over a little as he was walking and said, "Keep your head down, boys. There are German snipers on that ridge!"

Jack and Red looked at each other and smiled, realizing they needed to play along. Jack said, "Sergeant Rawlings, we are here to relieve you just as soon as you are ready to demobilize!"

All three of them were now crouched down as they walked around back to the old trailer. There was a wooden porch built against the front, and they walked along it to the other side. There in a shaded area, they saw the bike under an old, torn, tarp-like cover.

They pulled the cover back and saw the old World War II military scout. It was a drab, army gray and green, faded from time. Jack looked over and saw some old tools and some parts lying around. He said, "Henry, does this bike run?"

"I think so, but the tires went flat, and I think she's out of gas, and the spark plugs are fouled out." Henry then got on the bike and tried to kick it over, but he was not strong enough.

Red and Jack look at each other and grinned. Jack shook his head and said, "Sergeant, do you mind if we take a look at the bike? Maybe we can get her running."

"Sure, go ahead," he said. "I know that she'll run." His eyes light up with the excitement of a kid in a candy store.

Red walked over and grabbed one of the six packs and handed one to each of them. Then Henry walked over to the service station next door to get a tire pump. Red took it from him and started to pump up the tires.

Jack, in the meantime, pulled the plugs and scavenged through the tools. He found what he needed, and he started putting things back together.

After Red pumped up the tires, he grabbed a fuel can and walked over to the gas pump and bought four gallons of fuel. He dumped the fuel into the tank, and as he found the leaks, he tightened them up with a screwdriver.

Then Jack said, "Hey, Henry, okay if we give her a kick?"

"Sure, son. I know she will run. I know she'll run. She used to purr like a kitten!"

Jack looked at Red and said, "Well, turn her over slow. I'll put some oil in the cylinders, she might be stuck."

Red said, "You turn her over, and I will put the oil in the cylinders because I don't want to break anything."

Jack left the switch off and kicked her real easy a couple of times. Then he put the spark plugs back in and flipped the switch on. Red turned on the gas and pulled the choke. "Okay, Jack, jump on it!" You could hear the engine thump over and the pipes make a sound. *Bump, bump, bump, bump, bump,* and then, *bang!* A puff of smoke came out the exhaust pipes, and the engine jerked.

Henry was thoroughly excited. "You've got her going now, boys! She's like a woman. Push her hard, and she'll push right back to you!"

Red laughed and Jack jumped on it again. *Bump, bump, bump, bump, bump,* and she started to run slowly. The pipes spit out a little oil smoke as the engine started thumping and the pipes come to life. Jack twisted the throttle for a little bit more fuel, ever so gently then she started to smooth out a little. The bike continued to idle. As she warmed up the engine smoothed out and then Jack pushed the choke back off.

Jack motioned for Red to give him a screwdriver so he could adjust the fuel mixture.

Red came up and waved Jack's hand away so he could adjust the fuel mixture himself. And lo and behold, she started purring like a kitten.

Henry started singing and dancing all around the deck. He laughed, sang, and jumped up and down just like an old prospector who had just struck gold.

Jack yelled, "Hey, Henry, want me to run her around a bit?"

"Yes, son. Test her out! I knew she would run, I just knew it, by God!"

Jack rolled her forward, and she came off the stand. He then pushed up and down on the suspension. "She's a little stiff."

Red checked the tires and said, "Well, they're good, Jack."

Jack drove down the ramp and off the porch and took a run down the highway. He could feel the tires were a little flat from sitting for so many years as they thumped on the pavement. He rode her long and easy, slowly accelerating up while bringing her through the gears.

Suddenly the speedometer started to work. It was bouncing up and down, not quite steady at 65 miles an hour but working. Smiling, Jack thought, *This is totally awesome.* He ran her hard on the highway speeding up and down to make sure everything was working as it should. He rode for about another ten minutes and then turned back and pulled up and parked next to the trailer.

Henry said, "How did she run, Captain Jack?"

He smiled and said, "Very good, sir. You're ready!"

"Boy," he said, "I've been waiting a long time for you guys to show up! Hold on." He went into the trailer and came out wearing his old marine jacket and a military helmet.

"Boys," he said, "I will radio back when I get to the main base! I am finally going home, boys. Good luck to ya."

"Okay, Sergeant, but take her easy." Jack held the bike as it was still running and watched as Henry got on.

Henry put it into gear and went through the parking lot nice and easy and pulled up onto the highway. As he drove away, they could hear him shift through the gears just like he had gotten off that bike yesterday, and then he rolled out of sight.

Red and Jack put away the tools, washed their hands, and closed up the trailer.

Red said, "You think he's coming back?"

"Nope, I don't think so. Not today anyway, and if the big guy upstairs will watch over him, he is going to get to finally go home for good, I think."

Red stopped for a moment and said, "You know I never really thought of that."

Jack said, "Well, he did and he has been waiting for us for twenty years."

They walked back to their bikes, and Jack checked his watch. "We should roll."

They fired up their bikes and rolled through the parking lot. Jack looked over and saw the woman working in the liquor store looking out the window. She gave them the thumbs-up. Jack smiled and signaled back, and they both gave her a nod.

They pulled up on the highway and twisted the throttles down to full power. The pipes were screaming as the wind made them feel like they were flying.

Oh, Mexico

They reached the Mexican border through a farm road in Texas. A federali was sitting in a wooden chair with a bottle next to him. His eyes were closed, and he was sound asleep. They pulled their bikes up next to him, and the sound of the Harleys woke him. Jack handed him twenty American bucks. He grinned, leaned back, and waved them through as he closed his eyes again.

They rolled down a gravel road as the sun became a bright, orange ball just sitting in the western sky. Jack noticed a sign that pointed to a Highway Hotel and Cantina. Next to it was a lighted beer sign in Spanish.

They shifted their bikes down and the pipes thundered and moaned from the downshift as they rolled through the gravel parking lot and up to the Cantina.

They went around the building and pulled up on the side. They spotted Gussie's bike parked under a shade tree, so they drove up next to it and shut off their engines. Red said to Jack, "Well, it looks like old mad dog made it."

Jack smiled and said, "Well, he is here, so let's see what kind of shape he is in." They both got off their bikes, and Red moaned, "I am saddle sore."

Jack said, "Yea, that was an intense ride!" As they walked by the service station that was at the end of the building they notice Gussie lying on a rack of tires. He was face-up and the sun was beating down on him. His head hung down and his long, dirty, scraggily hair was almost touching the ground.

Jack walked up and shouted, "Hey, Gussi!" He thought his yelling would startle him, but Gussie didn't even flinch. He just lifted up his head and opened up one eye, but his eyes couldn't handle the bright sunlight so he closed them again and said, "What, Jack. I am trying to catch some Zs here, man."

Red said, "Man, you smell like dung! Did you do it in your pants? When was the last time you had a bath, man?"

Gussie moaned and in his scratchy voice said, "I don't know, why?"

"Because you smell like tequila and piss! That's why, man!" Red shouted.

He raised his head again, lifted up his arm, and smelled his armpit. Then said, "Yeah, I do need a bath!" Then he laid his head back down again. He was very drunk and hung over.

Jack said, "Are you going to sleep all day on that stack of tires or should we check you into a room?"

Red said, "I'll go check us in, but hey Gussie you're getting your own room!"

Gussie rolled slowly off the tires and stood up. He threw his long hair back and staggered toward Jack.

"Gussie!" Jack said.

"Yes, sir! Reporting for duty, sir!" He staggered as he tried to salute.

"Knock it off," Jack said. "Come on, let's get you to a room and get you a bath, Mr. Pig Pen."

Jack took the bottle out of his hand and threw it in the trash. He opened Gussie's jacket and pulled out two more bottles of whiskey and threw them in the trash as well.

Gussie said, "What the are you doing, Jack?"

"What you should've done a couple weeks ago. You stupid drunk!"

Gussie protested and said, "Come on, that was good booze!"

"Shut the hell up and come with me." Then Jack and Red each took one arm and walked him over to the hotel.

They all walked through the hotel lobby door, and a pretty, young Mexican girl with a beautiful smile said, "Buenos dias, gentlemen! How may I help you today?"

Gussie looked at her in a drunken stupor and said, "Only one of us is a gentleman. Can you guess which one?" Gussie started to fall down then caught himself on a free-standing wooden coat rack.

She blushed and said, "Oh no, senor, you are all gentlemen!"

He looked at Jack and said, "Hear that, Captain Jack. She actually thinks you're a gentleman!" He stumbled and fell backward onto a couch as Red just gave up trying to hold him and let him go.

Jack shook his head, and the girl looked at him with a question on her face. As he gave her the cash for the room, he said, "My friend and I need to get him cleaned up." Then pointed at Gussie who was now snoring on the coach.

She handed him a room key and helped Red and Jack pull Gussie up unto his feet. "Come on, Casanova. Let's get you into a shower. God, you stink! Did you pee in your pants all the way down here, or what?" Red said.

Gussie said, "Yeah, I think I did once or twice, not sure," as he tried to focus on Jack's face.

Jack opened the hotel door and pulled him into the room. He left Red holding him as he walked into the bathroom and started the shower. Jack walked back out and he and Red sat Gussie down on the bed. They proceeded to pull off his coat and boots.

"You're on your own with the rest your clothes."

Gussie got up and stripped naked and staggered into the shower. He stood there with the water pouring on his head.

Jack grabbed a bed sheet and threw his clothes in it and wrapped them up and walked back down to the front desk. He asked the girl, "Can you wash these?"

"No, Senor. No guest laundry. Just for hotel use."

Jack pulled out a couple of twenty-dollar bills and leaned forward and laid them flat on the desk and said, "Maybe now?"

She smiled and said, "Yes, sir. Right away, sir!"

Then he said, "You have a barber?"

She looked, "No compendia?"

He said, "Barber," and made a scissors motion with his fingers like he's cutting hair.

"Oh si, si, barber! Right away, sir. Yes, sir!"

She went in the backroom and said, "Mama" and he heard some of the words in Spanish, but he could not make them out. She came out with an older woman who said in a thick Spanish accent, "I can cut hair."

Jack nodded, and she walked up and started to touch Jack's hair. He said, "No, my friend, my amigo."

She said, "Okay, okay you bring a friend to me, yes?"

Jack said, "Wait one more momento!"

He walked back to Gussie's room and yelled, "Hey, still in the shower?" He opened the door to the bathroom and saw Gussie standing there, looking in the mirror and pulling on his long beard.

Jack said, "Well, you smell better, but you still look like garbage! Wrap that bath towel around you. I have to bring you to someone."

"No, Jack. No hookers, I'm too drunk. I won't be able to perform. Get them later, okay!"

Jack laughed. "Come on, you need a haircut and a shave." He wrapped the towel around himself and walked out behind Jack to the front desk.

"Okay," he said, "barber," and made the scissor motion again with his fingers.

The young woman behind the counter said, "Oh, yes, yes" and walked in the back room again. She came out and said, "Please, come," and motioned them to come on back.

They walked in and there was a chair in the middle of the storeroom. The older woman was standing next to the chair and had scissors and a comb in her hand. She motioned for Gussie to sit down. He slid into the chair, and she looked at him and smiled at the younger woman.

She had seen Gussie's big biceps and the marine tattoos on his arms. She said something in Spanish, and the two women giggled. Jack said to the woman, "Cut off his beard," and he put his hand to his face in a scissor motion. She nodded yes, and Jack walked back out to the front desk with the younger woman.

He said, "Can you get him dressed?"

"Oh, yes. Clothes ready when haircut is done."

"Okay then. Thank you!"

She said, "Thirty minute, he be ready."

Jack looked at his watch. "Okay, I will be back in thirty."

Jack spied the pay phone in the lobby and saw that Red was already talking. "Hey, Jack, do want to talk to Terri? She's awake!"

"Yes, I do!" He took the receiver from Red.

"Hello, Terri, is that you?

"Yes, Jack." Jack frowned, as her voice was very quiet, and she sounded very tired.

"Terri, are you doing better?"

"Yeah, but I'm sore and tired."

Jack said, "That's the drugs, honey. They'll knock you out."

"Yeah, I think she gave me more than I need."

"Oh, yeah. You think you don't need them, but you do. How are you and Donna getting along?"

"Oh, she's so nice. She's been helping me around. I think I've found a new friend."

"Yes, she's a good one."

"But she does not like being without Red though!"

"I know," said Jack.

"Hey, Jack."

"Yeah, Terri."

"Please be careful. I don't want to lose you!"

"Oh, I will, don't worry." He responded in a very calm and reassuring voice, so he would not make her worried.

"You have not called your mom, have you?"

"No, no, Jack, but I'm scared."

"Terri, I will make a quick call to your parents to let them know you're okay. I will call from a pay phone and will make it short so they can't trace it."

"Jack, don't tell them what happened. Mama will worry!"

"No, I will not tell them. Now you get some rest. You need to heal up, and I will see you soon."

Then Terri said, "Jack?"

"Yeah?"

"I know you have to do this, ah…whatever it is." She paused, and he could hear her crying softly.

Then he heard Donna on the phone. "She'll be okay, Jack. I am with her. You guys do what you have to do. Just come back to us in one piece. You got that!"

"Yes, I do, Donna. Just take good care of her, and I will bring Red back to you."

Jack hung up the phone and looked at Red. Then Red said, "We never thought we would have to call Broken Arrow after the war, did we?"

"No, Red, and I'm still not sure who our ultimate enemy is. Come on, let's go get Gussie." They walked back to the desk, and the woman was sitting there. Jack said, "Is our friend ready?"

"Oh, yes," and she went behind the wall and said some more Spanish words to her mother.

Gussie stepped out and saluted Jack and Red.

"Boy, you clean up good!" Jack said.

"Yes, sir! High and tight, just as you ordered!"

Red leaned over and gave him a smell. "Hey, is that French perfume?" The woman came out all smiles. "You like, amigos?"

"Yes, or gracias," said Jack, and he handed her a fifty-dollar bill.

"Thank you, senior. Nice to be of service to you!"

The guys laughed. "Come on, man. Let's get to the cantina and get some food." As they walked through the door, they saw a couple of locals at the bar and some families at the tables.

The waitress walked up to them and said, "Hi, guys, what will you have?"

Red looked at her and said, "Let me guess. You're from the Bronx, New York, right?"

"Yup, how did you guess?"

"I have been there a time or two."

She looked at all three of the guys and said, "Let me guess. You're on a bachelor's road trip, right?"

"Yes," said Jack, "our buddy here is getting married!"

Then she said, "Okay, who's really the groom?" She looked at Jack.

The other guys said, "Yeah, that's him. He is the groom!"

She laughed and said, "Three beers?"

Jack said, "Let's make them sodas instead."

Gussie, who was still feeling no pain, suddenly seemed much more sober.

The waitress looked at Gussie's bloodshot eyes and, smiling, said, "Oh, okay, three sodas coming up."

They looked at the menu that was mounted on the rack at the table, and Jack said, "Hey, it's all in Spanish."

Gussie said, "Flip it over, Sherlock. It's all in English on the flip side," and they all three laughed!

They ordered three steak dinners and ate their meals and made small talk about girls and bikes. Then Gussie said, "Okay, are the guys going to be at the location tomorrow?"

Jack said, "All but Dave and Donnie." Then he looked down at his soda and said, "It just doesn't seem right, does it, guys?"

"No, it doesn't," said Red. "How about Roscoe? Was he going to make it with his woman in that condition?"

"God, I hope so," said Jack, "but we're going to have to get her close to a doctor or midwife or something."

"Why doesn't he just take her to her folks in Texas?"

Jack said, "She can't go there. They know who she is and where they are. They will be watching them."

Gussie said, "Yeah, they might have them too!"

Jack looked over at him and said, "Well, I don't think they do, but I am sure they are watching them!"

Then Jack said, "I think Roscoe's got a plan worked out where he will take her, but it's best we don't know."

They all agreed. Then Gussie said, "Red where is your old lady?"

Red looked at Jack and then Jack said, "Ah she's with Terri back in Texas."

Gussie said, "Terri. Who the hell is Terri?"

Jack said, "Terri Thompson. Dave's little sister!"

"Well, what the heck is Dave's little sister doing in Texas with Donna?"

Jack and Red just kind of grin, then Gussie said, "Why didn't Roscoe come with you guys and leave his old lady back in Texarkana or that little jerk water town where he lives?"

Jack leaned back and ordered some coffee from the waitress and said, "Ah, we will be here awhile explaining this."

The Rendezvous

The sun rose early in the desert sky. It was a peaceful, quiet morning with only the occasional sound of a car or truck passing by. Gussie was up and ready to go, and he was pounding on Jack and Red's hotel door.

Red climbed out of bed and pulled the door open saying, "What do you want, Gussi!"

Then he noticed that Gussie had three large, foam cups of hot coffee.

"Come on; grab one, it's coffee time." He handed one to Red and walked over to Jack's bed and said, "Come on, biker boy," and handed him the other cup of coffee.

Jack said, "Boy, you sure are cocky when you're sober, aren't you?"

Then Gussie said, "All right, man, let's get moving. You guys want to get breakfast?"

"Yeah, we better fuel the hogs," said Red.

Gussie said, "I will meet you in the restaurant," and walked out of the room.

Jack and Red looked at each other and cracked up laughing! Jack said, "A new man just showed up," and they kept laughing. They sat down at the breakfast table, ordered some food, and put it down military style—fast, that is. When they were done, Jack said, "Okay, one day's ride left. Let's roll."

Gussie said, "Then what? Broken Arrow?"

"Yeah," Jack said.

"We need to surprise them and not just let them just follow us."

Gussie looked at him confused. "How are you going to pull that off if they are all ready on us? From what you told me last night they keep finding you!"

"Yes, you're right. No matter what we do, they keep finding us. But the best way to hunt bear is to have one chase you!"

Gussie looked at him smiled and nodded his head.

Red drank his coffee and looked up from the newspaper he was reading. "Oh that sounds smart! Do I have to remind you that you told us to ride bikes?"

Jack said, "Yeah I did, and so far that is working pretty well, right, Red? We are mobile as hell right now."

"Okay. You guys get ready I just need to load my saddlebags," said Red.

"Me too," said Gussi.

"We're good then. I will make a phone call and meet you guys at the bikes. Then we'll all ride straight to the location."

Red said, "All right vacation time," which caused Jack to roll his eyes.

"Oh yeah, it will be a great vacation!"

They were standing next to their bikes ready to go when Guzzi said, "Hey, that little senorita we saw last night looked pretty good. Was that the one that was behind the guest counter last night?"

Red said, "I think so. You recognize her now that your vision is not blurry! Otherwise you would have seen that last night!"

Jack said, "All right, come on, kids. Let's ride. This is going to be a very long day." Jack looked at Gussi. "I hope you're packing?"

He looked at Jack and rolled his eyes and said, "Well what do you think, Captain Jack? You think these bags are full of bottles?"

Red said, "Hey, I hope they're not full of bottles!"

Gussie said, "Yes, Molotov cocktails. Do you want me to light one for you?"

"No, thanks, I'm not thirsty right now," he said.

They kicked over the bikes, and the motors fired up. They put them in gear and slowly rolled through the parking lot and out onto the highway. As they thundered down the road, Jack took the lead and twisted the throttle on.

Running through the desert hard and fast, the ride became hot. Luckily they had not seen much for traffic. As they drove along, Jack noticed a small store and gas station up ahead at the base of the mountains.

He pointed for the guys to roll in and fuel up. A little Mexican kid about ten came out and walked up to them. "Okay, gringos, what will it be?"

Gussie cracked up laughing, and Red looked at Jack. He put his hands up, like, "I don't know about this kid." Gussie said, "Don't you mean, amigos?"

"No," he said, "I mean gringos!"

Jack said, "Fill them up. Here, better yet, let me fill them up!"

The kid turned on the high-test pumps. Jack said, "How old are you?"

"Ten, why?"

"Just asking."

Then the kid eyed up the bike and said, "Nice rides, man!"

Jack said, "Why is your English so good?"

"Texas!"

"What do you mean?"

"I am from Texas!"

Jack said, "Oh, well why do you live here in Mexico?"

The kid asked Jack as he was filling the bikes, "Why are you in Mexico?"

Jack said, "Well, you're a smart, little guy. Why do you think?"

"Oh, I'd say it's the law, drugs, or maybe both."

"Sorry to disappoint you there, partner, but it's not either one."

"So maybe not, but I bet it will be?"

"Why's that?"

"Because your friend has a gun barrel sticking out of his saddle bag!"

Jack hung up the pump, walked over, and looked at the saddlebag. He said, "There's no gun sticking out!"

The kid laughed. "But you have them with you, don't you?"

Jack said, "Hey, partner, didn't your parents ever teach you it's not a good idea to ask too many questions?"

"No, not really."

"Well, they should have," Jack said.

Then the kid said, "What's your name?" as he looked at Jack.

"Jack Monroe. What's your name?"

"Amelio." He stuck out his hand for a handshake.

"Well, it's nice to meet you, Amelio." They shook hands. Jack pulled out a roll of bills, and his eyes lit up.

"Ah, you pay me in American dollars?"

"Sure," Jack said. The kid pulled out a chart to convert the amount from pesos to American dollars and said, "Its $7.50 for all three bikes."

Jack looked at him. "Okay," and handed him a ten-dollar bill. The kid looked at his chart and started to count out the change in pesos.

Jack said, "Forget it. How about you keep the change?"

"All right. Hey, you are a nice guy, Jack."

"Well, thanks."

Then he handed Jack back his lighter and a wallet he had taken out of the saddlebag.

Jack said, "Well, you little thief!"

"Hey, I gave them back!" Then the kid took off running around the back of the store and disappeared. Just then Red and Gussie walked out.

Red yelled at Jack, "What's the total? We have to pay the lady."

Jack said, "No, we're good. I just paid the kid!"

"Oh," he said and walked back in the store. Then he came out again with an elderly Mexican woman behind him. He yelled over to the pumps, "Jack."

"What?"

"There is no kid working here. You have to pay the lady!"

Jack looked around and cracked up laughing.

Red said, "What's so funny?"

Jack walked up laughing and handed the woman another ten dollars. She looked at him puzzled and went inside to make change.

Red and Gussie said, "What the hell was that all about?"

Jack said, "Bandits. We just got held up by a little bandit!" Red and Gussie broke out laughing and then said, "Who was the kid?"

Jack responded as he was laughing, "A little bandit. I paid him for the gas at the pumps!"

They all continued to laugh, and then Red said, "You mean you gave your money to a kid who doesn't even work here?"

"Yeah," he said, "pretty good scam, huh?" They all got back on their bikes, and Jack hollered, "Let's ride."

Red said, "But what about your change, Jack?"

"Just forget the change!"

They rolled out onto the open highway and ran the bikes in single file. Each bike thundered as the exhaust pipes roared in a one-note song. Jack took the lead as they rolled over miles and miles of open country and desert highway. The sun was hot and beat down on them pretty good when Jack decided to play a game. He pulled a bottle of whiskey from his leather saddlebag, opened it up and passed it to the next rider. Then the guy in front dropped back and took the bottle. He took a sip and handed it to the next guy. They kept going back and forth drinking from the bottle and passing it back and forth like relay runners passing the baton.

The day rolled by, and the sun was blistering. The heat made the road look like a black, wavy stripe drawn through sand on a painter's canvas. When they reached the mountain they rode up a rough unpaved road to the rendezvous point. The bikes were hot from the desert heat and when they turned the bikes off, the pipes clicked and creaked as they began to cool down. The roar from the engines had now become silent, and they could hear a lone train whistle blowing from a far off track somewhere in the desert.

They parked next to each other as they looked out over the desert. You could see the faint blue of the ocean mixed with the horizon off in the distance.

Jack said, "Can you see it, gentlemen?" They nodded yes.

Gussie said, "Yeah, man, it is where yesterday and today meet."

Red said, "What, the horizon?"

"No, man," Gussie said. "Just the ocean, because today's water rolls back to yesterdays water!"

They all grinned, and Jack chuckled. "Gussie, you are a poet in your own right!"

Red looked at both of them and said, "Gussie, you are a poet, and you don't even know it!"

Gussie said, "Hey, you guys get away from me. You are messing up my chi." Then he walked away took off his shirt and flexed his muscles. He sat on a rock in a kind of yoga pose and started meditating.

Red and Jack looked at each other and shook their heads in bewilderment. They left Gussie to his meditation and started to walk down what looked like a rattlesnake trail. Jack stopped when he saw a very large diamondback snake shaking his rattle and putting his head back like he was ready to strike.

Jack slowly knelt down so he was face-to-face with the snake, and looked him straight in the eyes.

Red said, "What are you, nuts?"

Jack leaned forward, and the snake opened its mouth, exposed its fangs, and got ready to strike. Jack was on his knees with both hands on his hips and leaned in even farther with the snake. The snake continue to rattle and hiss at him, trying desperately to warn him to stay away.

Red said, "Hey, man, if he bites you, I am not sucking no poison out, so back off."

Jack continued to stare down the snake eye-to-eye then he winked his left eye, and suddenly the snake dropped his tail and slid off into the brush. Jack stood up and brushed off his knees. He turned and looked at Red, who had his .45 out and pointed.

He looked at Jack and said, "Man, he was actually scared of this gun!"

Jack said, "Yeah right, he knew exactly what a .45 auto was." Red shook his head and clicked the safety back on, and they walked back to the bikes.

Jack walked over and lay back on some rocks, feeling their warmth from the sun. He could hear the highway below. He felt the cars go by, pushing the wind, and listened to their tires whine on the hot desert pavement.

As he lay there, looking into the sun, a young hawk flew over, soaring in a circle around him. He looked over at the ocean, and the sun was touching the water in a beautiful display of colors.

He heard Red walk up the trail toward him. Red said, "Where's camp tonight, Captain?"

"Right here!"

"What? Aren't we going into Desert Rose to meet the guys?"

"No, they are coming this way up the mountain. We will see them soon enough."

Then Red said, "How about we hear them first?"

Jack said, "Oh yeah, with those hogs, we should be hearing them first." Just then they heard the sound of choppers coming up the rough mountain road. They could make out the first bike and see it was Roscoe on his custom hog leading the pack. They thundered up the road to the top of the mountain where they were standing. In order, each one pulled up alongside of the other bike and shut off his engine and put the kick-stand down.

One by one, they got off, stretched, and rubbed the parts of them that were sore. It was silent at first; they just looked at each other and nodded. The whole group looked over at Jack, who nodded and pointed to a clearing behind some rocks. "We'll make camp here."

They looked at him and smiled, and then they rolled their bikes to a flat and secluded area behind some trees. They all pulled off their packs and bags from the bikes and spread out, making camp. Red said, "Just like old times, eh, Captain!"

Jack laughed and said, "Yeah, no matter how old we get, we still like playing army!"

Then Ringo said, "Army, that's just boy scouts! I thought we were playing marines and special ops kind of guys!"

Gussie, who was still kind of mad because he was not going to be able to party in Acapulco said, "Whatever, it's all fun! Eh!"

Roscoe said, "Hey, Gussie, do you have a scorpion up your butt, or are you just happy to see us?"

"Oh, screw you, guys," he said, "I'm bedding down! I'm tired!"

Jack said, "That would be best for all of you. I am going to go over some plans. We will mobilize at sunrise."

Then they all said, "Yes, sir, Captain Jack!"

"Oh, knock it off. Talk to you in the morning."

They all kind of laughed and got comfortable. Jack walked over to a little clearing and sat down on some rocks and, taking a stick, started scratching in the sand. He looked over and saw they had a small fire burning and were all talking. Each one was looking up at the stars while lying on their backs.

Jack got up and walked over. "Hey, guys, put the fire out!"

Red said, "Why?"

Jack snapped back. "Because we are going to have company tomorrow, and let's hope they don't locate us tonight before we are ready for them!"

Gussie got up and kicked out the fire and said, "Yeah, what were you guys thinking? I will take the first watch," he said. Gussie moved over to the rocks overlooking the road coming up to the mountain.

Jack said, "Then you guys need to—"

But before he could finish, Red said, "Jack, we know the plan and the order for the watch and rotation."

"Oh yeah, right," he said. "Well—"

And again before he could finish, Red said, "Calm down, man, we've got you covered."

"Yeah, okay." He walked over to a patch of sand and looked at his map. He glanced up at the stars and thought, *I got them home from the war, and I hope I don't get them killed in Mexico.* Then he bowed his head and said a silent prayer.

He looked up again and could see the distant light of the town Desert Rose and heard an occasional car and truck pass by the road at the base of the mountain. Jack put his boot down in the middle of the map and then scratched away the lines in the sand. He got up to check on Ringo, who was keeping watch at the point.

"You okay there, man?"

"Yeah," Ringo said. "Why wouldn't I?"

"Oh, I know you are okay."

Ringo said, "What's bothering you, Jack?"

"I am not sure yet, but I know it will come to me."

He looked at Jack and said, "You don't really have plan, do you?"

"No, I don't. But I am sure they will know we are here."

Ringo said, "Yeah, you're right. They will be here, and we will make it up as we go. We always do, right?"

Jack smiled and said, "I will talk to you in the morning."

Jack pulled out an M-16 from Red's weapon bag and went down the snake trail to keep watch on the back side. He heard an owl hoot and a coyote celebrate his kill.

He was looking at the gun and noticed the initials of someone he did not know carved in the gun.

He thought when Red bought this from that sur-plus dealer, *I wonder if he even knew who this gun belong to, or if he wondered, did this guy even make it home?*

The night toiled on. The wind had picked up a little and the breeze felt good on his face. He could hear the guys whisper as they each got up after taking his three-hour shifts at watch.

Jack stayed up all night watching over them; he looked up and noticed that the sun was starting to climb in the morning sky. Another day.

Anything Goes When Everything is Gone

It was daybreak on the mountain and all the guys were up and rustling around. They were packing their things into their bags when Jack walked over to them and said, "I have coffee in my pack. You guys want some?"

"Yeah, oh, yeah," they all responded in unison. He laughed and started the small propane torch heater to boil the water. Red pulled out some bread rolls from his pack and threw one to each of the guys. They each took the metal cups from their mess kits and got their morning coffee.

They sat in a circle on a pile of rocks, sipped their coffee, and they all stared at Jack, hoping to hear one of his brilliant military plans.

Jack looked at them and said, "I am not sure what to expect here."

They looked at him confused. This was not the Captain Jack they knew. They kept quiet and waited patiently for more information. Jack said, "These guys are after a book. It has information covering illegal dealings from the war. They know one of us has it. They thought Dave had it, but he didn't. Then I think they thought Donnie Boscoe had it, and I am sure they killed him trying to find it.

"Now we are down to five guys left, and one of us has it. I am not sure why, but one of us has it. I can only assume at this point they will kill us all to get it."

Red said, "I assume the info in this book is something they don't want the public to know?"

Jack said, "I have not seen it, but that is what I would assume. It's the real reason we were in Vietnam in the first place. What I need know is, do one of you have this book?"

They were quiet, and they each started to look at each other. There was a long pause amongst them.

Then Gussie said, "I got it!"

They all looked at him, and Jack said, "Where did you get it?"

"Remember that whorehouse in Saigon that we used to go to?"

"Not really," Jack said, "but what about it?"

"Well," he said, "couple of operatives were seeing the same two girls I was. They used to meet and exchange information there every week."

Jack said, "In a whorehouse? How do you even know that?"

"Well, one night I had both girls giving me a bath when this guy comes in all pissed off because I had bought both girls for the night so he couldn't have them. He was drunk and an American, clean cut, but not military.

He was looking for the girls because he had promised them to his buddies as some sort of debt repayment.

He was raising so much ruckus with the madam and pushing the doorman around that I had to get out of the bathtub and beat his butt.

The madam was scared of him, so she asked me to throw him out on the street. He must have had this book in his coat pocket and lost it in the shuffle. One of the girls picked it up and gave it to me."

Jack said, "Any idea who this guy was?"

"Yeah. The girls told me he was a US senator and that he came in once a month to meet these CIA guys and get a little stress relief."

Jack said, "Well, that explains a lot. This is much deeper than we could have imagined."

Red said, "You know, we always had the plan that if one of us was in trouble from the things that happened in the war, we would call Broken Arrow and meet at Desert Rose. The bad guys know this, don't they, Jack?"

"Yeah, they do. That was why we are expecting them here."

Gussie said, "How do they know that?"

"I am not sure exactly," said Jack, "but it may have come from Dave."

"No way," said Red, "Dave Thompson would never give up that information."

"Well, maybe he didn't."

"Well, then how do they know?"

"Terri."

"Man," said Gussie. "Why would she tell them?"

"Because they have her folks, and she is afraid they might kill them. So when she would call them each night to say she was all right, she actually was telling them where we were and where we were going. She knew the last time she called I was going to take her to Mexico. Dave had always told her that someday they would take a vacation to this beautiful, out-of-the-way town called Desert Rose."

The guys all shook their heads, and Roscoe said, "Don't tell me we are just going to ride into town and take on God knows what or who without any plan!"

Jack said, "Well, they think we have the book. So if we give it to them, they will let Mr. and Mrs. Thompson go."

Roscoe said, "What if they kill them and all of us as well?"

Jack sighed and said, "If they think we have a copy of the book, they will not be so eager to do that until they know we cannot go public. It just may give us some time to get to them first. They are not going to stop guys until we stop them."

The guys all shook their heads in agreement.

Jack said, "We have to end this fight, and we have to do it here today. No matter what it takes, we end this today. Agreed?"

In unison they shouted, "Agreed. Who yah!"

They all got up and headed to their bikes. They readied their bags and tied them on. Each one of them went through his own ritual to start their bikes.

Red shouted over to Jack, "Who are these guys exactly?"

Jack responded, "Wolves a pack of wolves!"

Red said, "Yeah, of course. I am going to hunt a whole pack of wolves!"

They rolled down the mountain in formation, side by side with Jack in the lead. It sounded like rolling thunder with the chrome and the steel sending flashes of lighting streaking across the ground. The group of Harleys made a wind as they passed small ranches and little shacks along the hot, dry, sandy mountain road. As they approach the city, they saw the blue tint of the ocean ahead of them. They rolled onto Main Street in front of a hotel and restaurant. Two of the guys moved to a spot across the street and Jack parked out front with the other two. He looked at Gussie and said, "You have the book with you, right?"

"Yeah, man, I have it!"

"That's good," Jack said, "because we have a fifty-fifty chance of getting out of here alive as it is."

Gussie said, "I said I would give it to them, didn't I?"

"Yes, you did, but I know you have changed your mind from time to time."

They were silent as they sat on their bikes, waiting on trouble and the morning sun to rise up all the way. A few local farm trucks rolled in and started unloading their goods for the street market that was about to open. A couple of young boys were chasing chickens that had gotten loose and were laughing as they ran in circles after them.

Gussie looked at Jack. "Hey, how far does this thing go up anyway?"

He responded, "Not sure, but I am thinking it went as far as it can."

Gussie said, "Are they going to show up in standard, four-door sedans and a van with shooters like they did in the other countries?"

"Not sure. I am thinking they may change their tactic a little considering they have lost enough guys at this point."

"Yeah," he said, "sounds like you opened up a can of whoop-em!"

Jack looked over at him and smiled. "Hey, you see that farm truck over there?"

"Yeah, why?"

Jack said, "Well about a dozen trucks came in and unloaded and that one came in never unloaded. It's just sitting there."

"Oh yeah" said Gussie, "Can you see how many guys are sitting in it?"

"Two, I think, but I can't tell if they are big or small, young or old because of all the Mexican garb!"

Gussie said, "Did you notice the other Mexicans were not dressed like that?"

Jack said, "I guess these guys are not from around here."

Gussie said, "I bet it is a truck full of guys and that is their fire power."

Jack said, "Are they looking over here at us?"

Gussie slowly pulled down his sunglasses a bit and looked over the top of them. "Yeah, the driver has his eyes glued on us, and the passenger is looking down the alley. Looks like he is watching to see if anyone comes out from between the buildings."

Jack said, "Look over there. Do you see the dust from a car coming down from the mountain road?"

"Yeah," said Gussie, "It looked like they found our camp last night and are heading here."

Jack said, "That's about right, but my guess is the kingpin is going to show up from the air."

"A chopper?" Gussie asked.

"Yeah. They most likely will have Terri's parents with them unless they already killed them."

"No" said Gussie, "They won't do that because they are going to want to trade for the book."

Jack said, "I hope you're right because they have no leverage otherwise."

"Unless they have the Federalis backing them, they may plan to take us out," Gussie said.

Gussie kept his eye on the car that was speeding toward the city while Jack kept a lookout in the sky for a chopper. They heard a whistle and looked to see Red behind some crates and pallets. Red signaled to watch the back of the farm truck. Jack gave him a nod.

Jack looked around and spotted Ringo and Roscoe under the truck and wiring explosives. The guys sitting inside the truck had no clue as to what was happening underneath them.

Red was at his post along the building. He was seated on the crates with his M-16 poised and ready along with a sniper rifle tripod.

Jack said, "You notice everyone has left the street."

Gussie said, "Yeah, it's very quiet." He saw the locals peeking out the windows.

"Hey, the locals know what's about to go down and maybe who is going to bring it!"

"Yeah" said Gussie, "they sure as hell do."

"Should we take cover?"

"No, we are the point men on this. I am sure it is supposed to be an exchange at first, and then they will try to screw us over."

The town had a town square with a big clearing that was located at the intersections of four streets. They kept their eyes on the town square and saw two more sedans pull up, one in front and one in back of the first sedan. Jack could not tell who was inside or how many were in any one of the cars. He saw that Ringo and Roscoe were set up along the farmer's market area, and all the rifles were sighted toward the square along with Jack's M-16.

Gussie said, "Well, we are smart to stay off the roof tops because if they come by chopper they will spot us. Should we signal Ringo and Roscoe to rig the cars to blow just like the truck?"

"No, man. We don't know who is in those cars. It may be Terri parents."

"Yeah, I suppose you are right."

Right then they heard the sound of a helicopter. As it came into sight, Jack noticed that all the windows were black tinted so you couldn't see in.

The chopper made one pass around the city, passing over where Jack and Gussie sat on their bikes. Then it swooped down and landed in the square. As the rotors winded down, Jack and Gussie took their side arms off safety. They each had two .45 automatics in the back of their pants underneath their leather jackets. They got off the bikes, and Jack slipped the M-16 back into the saddlebag. Gussie took out the book, and he and Jack started to walk toward the chopper. Gussie said in a low voice, "You still got a backup piece in your boot, Jack?"

"Yeah, as always, and a couple of throwing knifes for good measure."

As they approached the chopper, the door opened, and a big guy in a grey suit and reflective sunglasses stepped out. He had an earpiece and an automatic rifle in his arms. He stood right in front of them so they wouldn't come any closer. Jack saw another guy get out who was the same size and even a little uglier than the first guy. He stood just a few steps apart from the first guy.

Then a third guy got out. He was tall, wearing an expensive suit and shades. He had grey hair and Jack thought he was a politician for sure.

Jack whispered to Gussie, "Is that the senator from the whorehouse?"

"Yes, sir. Can I kill him?"

"Don't make any moves, Gussie, until we know we have Terri's parents."

"Then can I kill him?"

"Wait until I tell you!"

"Okay, on standby," Gussie said.

The senator continued to walk toward them. He passed through his two goons and said, "Well, Captain Jack Monroe!"

Jack said, "Do we know each other?"

"No, we have never met, but I have heard all about you!"

"Really," said Jack. "Well don't believe everything you hear!"

He said, "I am Senator Davis from the great state of Alabama!"

Jack said, "Is that supposed to impress me?"

"Look, son," he said in an angry voice, "you don't know what you're dealing with here."

Jack looked at his goons and said, "Maybe not, but one thing was for sure, you have no idea who you are dealing with either!"

After that remark, the two goons started to walk up to Jack. Jack said, "You back the dumb muscle up, or I'll kill them where they stand!"

The senator motioned the goons to back away. He could see that Gussie's trigger finger was getting itchy!

"Do you have what I have been looking for, son?"

Jack said, "You know, we were never told what you were looking for."

The senator smirked and said, "But you knew, didn't you, soldier?"

Jack said, "Where are Mr. and Mrs. Thompson?"

The senator looked at the chopper and gave the signal for them to come out.

They came out, and Jack cringed as he could see that they had been roughed up a bit. Mrs. Thompson looked like she was in shock, and she was crying.

"Now you give me the book, son, and I release them to you."

Jack said, "They walk across the street right now to that hotel, and then we will continue to talk."

He nodded yes, and the goons took off their handcuffs. Crying, Mrs. Thompson said, "Jack," and the goon pushed her away. They stood there for a few minutes. The chopper still had its motor idling, and the blades were barely turning. They watched as the Thompson's walked over into the hotel.

"Now," said the senator. "Can I see my book?"

Jack looked over at Gussie, who reached inside his jacket. The goons quickly aimed their weapons at him.

"Easy," said Jack. Gussie continued to put his left hand inside to his jacket pocket and pulled out the book.

It was an old, worn, leather book with hand scribbles all over the pages. The senator smiled and said, "Hand it over to me, son." He put his hand on the end of the book and pulled on it, but Gussie wouldn't let go.

Gussie said, "What are the odds that you just are going to let us walk away from here?"

He said, "Zero if you don't give me that book!"

Gussie said, "You know how many men died in Vietnam?"

The senator just stood there and held onto the book. Then Jack said, "Do you know how many were wounded and came back with parts of them missing?"

"Maybe we should just kill you now," said Gussie.

With a cocky grin, the senator said, "I don't think so, soldiers. Not until you get the women back."

This tripped Jack's trigger. He was so angry that the veins were standing out on his neck. He said, "Where are they?"

"Well, they are right here!" He pointed over to the car in the middle and made a signal. The back door opened, and a guy in a black, leather jacket got out.

He then reached in and pulled Terri and Donna out. Terri yelled, "Jack, please, Jack!" The goon then pushed both her and Donna back in the car.

Jack looked out of the corner of his eye and saw that Red had his rifle sighted on the middle sedan. Gussie released the book, and the senator grabbed it. Then Jack said, "How do you know that we did not make a copy of that?"

"I am going to assume you did! We are going to keep your ladies for thirty days. During that time we will release a story to the press identifying you guys as a threat to national security and wanted for war crimes in Southeast Asia. You will have to leave the country, never to return. We of course will have you followed for the rest of your life, and if a copy of this book ever surfaces, we will kill all of you, your families, and anybody you ever knew. I will release the ladies unharmed after thirty days, but you will be out of the country—all of you! You can stay here if you like, but mark my words, you cross that border, and we will cut you up and feed you to the sharks."

Gussie gave Jack that look like he was going for his gun, and Jack gave him a slow nod to stand down. Gussie relaxed a bit and said. "You know, Senator, every one of you guys are scumbags. It was my honor to serve my country, but you are not part of my country, you piece of crap!"

With a real cocky smirk, he replied, "Sticks and stones, son. Sticks and stones. You bottom feeders don't even know who owns this country. We do! The ones with money and the power. We have expendable soldiers like you to fight the wars so we can get more money and more power!" At that, he turned and started to get in the chopper and said, "Thirty days, Jack, the girls will be released in Dry Run, Texas in thirty days, but you better not be within a hundred miles of that border." He then he got into the chopper and the two goons got in behind him. The door closed, and the blades started to wind up. Jack looked at Red and gave a nod. Red fired a round and hit the chopper in the rear rotor, and it started to smoke and spin around.

Jack and Ringo hit the deck. A couple of sniper shots were fired, which barely missed them as they took cover behind the Mexican war memorial. Then the farm truck with a goon squad in it came to life. The dozen or so men started to climb out when Ringo pushed the switch and—*Boom!* A huge fireball erupted, and the truck flipped through the air and exploded!

Some of the men were crawling away from the fire, which made them an easy target for Roscoe to pick them off one by one. *Bang! Bang!* They dropped as he shot. Parts of them flew off, and blood was everywhere. A few people from the town were now screaming in Spanish to run away. The sedans pulled out from the curb, and Red shot the tires out of the first one. It spun out on the main street and crashed into a wall. The guys got out and crouched behind the car doors for protection.

They fired randomly, not knowing where the shots were coming from. The second sedan drove up on the curb and down the sidewalk, smashing vendor carts, flowerpots, and anything in its way. Red couldn't get a clear shot at the tires without risking hurting the girls inside, so he stopped firing.

Red yelled to Ringo, who was down the sidewalk behind the post, "Take the rifle," and pointed at the third car that was trying to get away.

Ringo was on it and unleashed hell on the third sedan. It spun around in the street and drove through the square. Jack stood up with Gussie, who yelled, "Jack, go for the girls. I got these guys!"

Jack ran for his bike through a hail of bullets. One grazed his cheek, and blood started to run down his face. He jumped the bike and shifted through the gears fast and hard.

He rode up a wooden ramp and through the loading dock in the market. He flew across the concrete and off a loading ramp. He cleared a railroad track and took off after the second sedan!

He heard another bike along side of him and looked over to Red, who was giving it everything the bike had as they chased down the sedan.

Gussie had taken out the driver of the third sedan as they were still trying to get away with the tires shot out. The wheels were on fire when it finally crashed into a power pole, which fell onto a building. The building started on fire and the car burst into flames. Gussie, crouched down with a pistol in his left hand and one in his right, was still firing away. He hit one of the guys from the first sedan and one from the third who had started running down the street. *Bang!* The shot hit him in the back of the head.

Guzzie, lay down flat with no cover and took one in the leg. "Ah geez!" he yelled, "Ringo, Roscoe, get these guys. I'm hit!"

He rolled over to see Rosco run up to the first sedan with three guys. They were shooting at him and Roscoe shot two of them before he got hit in the shoulder. Taking the bullet, he rolled over behind some crates for cover. The other two guys jumped out of the burning car and ran into the hotel. The other shooter from first car was still shooting, using the car as cover.

When bang, Ringo fired a shot. Perfect shot. The shooter's head exploded. Ringo yelled out, "Pop, goes the weasel!"

The helicopter still sat on the edge of town, trying to get up, when the pilot finally gave up and set it down in the street. Gussie crawled over to a park bench by some trees. He was bleeding profusely, so he tore his shirt bottom off and wrapped the bullet hole in his leg.

The shooting had stopped for a few minutes. Gussie yelled, "Roscoe, you hit?"

"Yeah, but I'm okay!"

"Ringo?"

"No, man, not a dang scratch!"

"Good, where is Red?"

"He hauled butt after his woman," said Ringo.

"How about Jack? Did he get after the sedan?"

"Yes!"

Gussie said, "Ringo, there are two in the hotel, and the chopper is down at the end of the street. Ringo, you go get the two in the hotel."

"Why me?"

"Because you're not shot! You dumb hillbilly, now get moving!"

"Yeah, I'm on it!" Then he yelled back, "Hey, Gussie!"

"Yeah?"

"Don't kill all them in the chopper. Save a couple for me."

Gussie rolled his eyes and said, "Just get moving before you lose them!"

"Yes, sir."

"Rosco, can you run?"

"Yeah!"

"Can you shoot?"

"Yeah!"

"Then run down the street and shoot those other two guys would you?"

"Yeah!" He could see Roscoe run down the sidewalk.

Guzzie managed to stand up and hobble through the square. He took cover behind the monument and reloaded his weapons. He then started to work his way down the street. He could see the smoke from the chopper that was now in flames. As he walked along the street, he heard a crash from the hotel and saw one of the bad guys flying out of the second story window on fire. Then he heard a shot and a crash, and the second guy flew out another second story window. He landed on his feet and broke his legs. He screamed and tried to crawl away. Then Ringo ran out on the street and shot them both with an M-16.

"Hey, Gussie! I got them!" he shouted.

Gussie again rolled his eyes and yelled back, "I see that. Now get yourself down this way!"

"Okay." He came on a dead run.

Gussie said, "Can you see down there? Are those guys from the chopper in that building, or what?"

"I don't know. I will have to sneak up on them."

"Okay, but move slow. I will come up and keep you covered. Those goons have autos. I hope Roscoe got those two guys down the street."

"I didn't hear any shots." Just then, they heard, *Bang! Bang!* And then silence. They looked at each other. "Yup, he found them!"

A few moments later, Roscoe came right up behind them. Gussie said, "You scared the daylights out of me! Are they done?"

"Yeah. They are not going anywhere. Don't worry!"

"How did you find us?"

"Easy, you're leaving a blood trail."

He looked down and realized he was still bleeding hard. Roscoe ripped his shirt apart and made a better bandage.

He pulled it tighter for more direct pressure and said, "You're going to have to leave the SOB to us. You sit here and take cover."

Gussie had two M-16s. "Here, take one of these."

"Hey, Gussie," Roscoe said, "it's good to fight with you and the captain again. Just like old times." He smiled.

Gussie nodded and sat back to catch his breath.

Jack and Red are up on the bumper of the sedan speeding down a gravel road. The guy in the passenger side continued to fire out the window, but they kept bobbing and weaving the bikes from side to side to keep away from the line of fire. Rocks and debris from the road way flew up and beat the hell out of them. The car kept fish tailing in the loose gravel. Through the back window, they saw Donna and Terri. They still had their hands tied and duct tape across their mouths. They were looking back, trying to see Jack and Red behind them. The speed kept getting faster, and it was all they could do to keep the bikes on the loose gravel. They each tried to get on the side of the car, when the car swerved over and tried to knock the bikes off the road. They were going over bumps and hills that caused the car and the bikes to go airborne.

Up ahead was a bus full of field workers who were getting out to work in the field. The bus was took up most of the road. The car tried to pass the bus but didn't make it. It hit the left rear corner which caused the car to flip up onto its side. The impact was so great that it pushed the bus forward a few feet.

Glass shattered all over, and the passengers in the bus were thrown forward and knocked down. The car slid on its side into the field and rolled over onto its roof. The two motorcycles barely missed the bus and slid to a stop next to the car. Jack and Red jumped off their bikes and dropped them just where they were. They immediately drew their guns.

Jack took the passenger side, and Red took the driver's side. They crouched down and looked into the car. At that moment the passenger fired a shot that just missed Red's foot.

Red fell flat and looked into the car. The guy in the passenger seat was all busted up and had a very shaky and bloody hand, but he was still tried to take aim again. *Bang!* Red put one between his eyes.

Jack checked the driver. He was already dead. His neck was broken. Jack nodded to Red, and they pulled the back doors open. Red grabbed Donna and pulled her out. She is shaken up and beat up but okay.

She threw her arms around Red and began to cry. Red held her as Jack crawled into the back seat and pulled Terri out. She also was quite shaken and cut up but awake. Jack pulled off her duct tape and untied her hands. Terri was also crying and her voice was scratchy as she said, "trunk," and pointed. Jack reached into the car and took the keys out of the ignition.

He opened the trunk and saw the doctor. He reached in and pulled her out. She was dead. Her neck was broken from the car rolling over. Jack gently laid her down, and the Terri and Donna knelt down next to her and sobbed.

Red said, "Are you sure she is gone?"

"Yeah," Jack said as he checked her pulse and listened to her heart. He closed her eyes and took off his jacket to cover her face.

Just then the workers from the bus came up and started to pray for her soul. They asked the girls if they were okay. The women workers checked them out to make sure. They looked at the guys who were dead in the car and said in broken English, "These are bad men, yes?"

"Yeah, bad men," said Jack. They nodded, and Jack said to Donna and Terri, "Can you girls ride?"

They nodded yes, and they then got on the bikes and headed back to town. They rolled onto Main Street and saw the helicopter burning and a car in the street on fire. Dead bodies were lying everywhere, some of them burnt. They had to cover their noses due to the smell of burning flesh.

The locals were still hiding in the buildings, and occasionally they could see one peeking out the windows. They took the girls to the hotel and told them to find Terri's parents. Terri, with tears in her eyes, took off in a dead run. She was anxious to find her parents. Red and Jack parked their bikes along the street and walked down toward the helicopter.

They found a blood trail and drew their weapons. Following it carefully, it led them to some crates where they found Gussie with a rag wrapped around his leg.

Jack said, "How bad is it?"

"Don't know for sure, but I will make it. Did you get the girls?"

"Yeah, we got them. They are okay."

Gussie, out of breath from the pain, said, "Good."

"We got them all but the two goons, the senator, and the pilot, we are not sure where they went. Go get them, Captain," Gussie said with a tired voice.

Jack nodded. "Lie low. We'll get out of here soon."

Red clicked in a new clip and loaded one in the chamber then said, "Where are Ringo and Roscoe?"

"Roscoe was hit in the shoulder, but it's not bad, so he went down the street with Ringo. I was just keeping post here. I can't do much else," Gussie said.

Jack said, "All right, let's end this thing!"

Gussie said, "Hey, Jack?"

"Yeah?"

"Remember what that scumbag said to us?"

Jack nodded his head, and he and Red took off down the street.

They came up on the burning chopper. Red snuck up and looked in the cab and held his nose. He ran back to where Jack was waiting. "Well, I know where the pilot is. That's one down."

Jack said, "Extra crispy, I bet."

"Yeah, that's an understatement."

They walked into the warehouse and saw the silhouette of a man standing between some packaging machines. Red pointed at Jack and motioned to cover him. When he got close, he could tell it was Ringo, so he made a bird call. Ringo waved him over. Ringo whispered, "We've got one of the goons hiding in that freezer over there and Roscoe is up on that mezzanine waiting for him to come out."

"Where is the other goon and the senator?"

"I think the other goon is in here, but the senator may have gotten out and went back toward the town square."

"Okay. Hold tight I will be right back," Red said.

Red ran back to where Jack was waiting and said, "They've got one goon hiding in the freezer and the other one might be downstairs."

Jack said, "Where is the senator?"

"He thinks he got out of the warehouse and went down the street toward the town square."

"Hell!" said Jack, "I will take the senator. Can you get these guys, Red?"

"No worries, do you want them alive for any reason?"

He looked at Red. "Can't think of any."

"Okay, got it." He headed back in.

Red told Ringo, "You signal Roscoe to keep a bead on that freezer door and you cover me as go out the back."

"What are you going to do?"

"Smoke him out of there. Watch for his buddy!" Red said.

"Yeah, got it!"

Red went out back and found a ladder going up to the roof and climbed up. Once on top, he found where the refrigeration compressor and the supply duct that led down to the freezer. The unit was running, so he carefully lifted off the side panel. He tore off the cover's insulation and rolled it up. He then took his lighter and lit it on fire and shoved it in the air supply and snapped the cover back on.

In a few minutes, he heard three shots. *Bang! Bang! Bang!*

He smiled and said, "One down!" He came down from the roof and went back into the warehouse and found Ringo. He nodded and pointed. Lying in front of the freezer door was goon number one with three shots in him. He looked over at Roscoe, who was still at ready, and gave him the thumbs up!

He nodded and motioned to bring him another target.

Red went back over to Ringo and whispered, "How do I get downstairs? Unless you want to go down stairs, Ringo?"

He whispered back, "No, man. You're better at this stuff than me. You go."

Red shook his head and walked over to the dark corner of the room where the stairs led to the basement. He readied his weapon and started down the stairs. There was very little daylight coming into the space. The basement was full of old animal hides and leather working equipment. Red walked carefully through the stacks of hides and tried to make out any movement. He has now reached the other side of the room from the stairs when he heard a radio squawk, "Come in. Over."

The radio noise was just in front of him. Red fired and heard things fall over crashing and clunking as someone ran up the stairs. Then he heard three consecutive shots! *Bang! Bang! Bang!*

Red walked to the stairs, looked up and yelled, "Ringo!"

"Yeah!"

"Red!"

"Yeah!"

"Is the target down?"

"Yeah!"

"Good. I am coming up," Red shouted.

Red, Ringo, and Roscoe headed outside and walked back to where they had left Gussie. As they approached Gussie they noticed that he was slumped forward with his head down. Ringo said, "Gussie, what the hell, man!"

"You fell asleep on us." He tipped his head back and stood up when he saw the bullet hole through his forehead!

Roscoe said, "Those scumbags," and he closed Gussie's eyes.

Red said, "We must have one more shooter, and he's moving down the street."

Ringo was in a trance staring at Gussie. Red whispered, "Ringo! Ringo! Come on, you can't help him now. He is gone. Stay with us, Ringo."

Ringo got up, bent down again, and put his hand in Gussie's boot.

"What are you doing?" said Red.

Ringo pulled out a throwing knife and put it in his back pocket. They moved down the street, looking around, checking in doorways, and coming upon a few locals who were terrified!

In total silence, they made their way to the hotel. They heard nothing. They all started checking the rooms. When they opened one of the doors, they saw a Mexican family all huddled together, shivering in fear. The parents had a firm grip on the children, trying to protect them from any impending harm. Red said, "Did you see"—and pointed his fingers to his eyes—"amigo like me?"

They shook their heads yes and pointed down the hall.

Red whispered, "Ringo, get them out of here." Ringo nodded and picked up the little girl and motioned for the family to follow him. He took them out the front door. Roscoe and Red whispered, "Where the hell is Jack?"

They kept moving along the hallway until they heard a whimper coming from a room. They each took a position on each side of the doorway then Red reached over and opened the door. They saw Mrs. Thompson. She was beaten up pretty bad and was tied to a chair. Roscoe stepped in and pulled off her gag. "Where are they? Do they have more men?"

"Four more guys are here in the hotel. They took Terri and Donna down the street! Where is Jack?"

"He went after them."

"Where is your husband?" Red asked.

She started to sob and motioned out the window. Red went to the window and saw him lying facedown in the street in a pool of blood. They untied her, and Red said, "Roscoe get her out of here and go find Ringo and tell him to protect her."

She said, "Please, oh God, please. Don't let them hurt my Terri."

Red nodded. "Keep her out of sight!"

Red put a new clip in the M-16 and readied both pistols again. He headed down the street when he saw a Mexican policemen hiding out front of a hardware store with his gun drawn. Red looked at him, and he nodded and pointed inside. Red crouched down and crawled along some shelving full of tools. He saw two of the guys beating a local for information. He put his

M-16 on single fire and popped the first guy in the head. *Bang!* Blood flew all over the second guy, who looked up, drawing his weapon.

Too late. *Bang!* Red shot him between the eyes. He untied the local guy and said, "Do you speak English?"

The local guy shook his head yes!

Red said, "Where are the women?"

He pointed down the stairs. Red headed down the stairs and heard the women whimpering. They were tied up and sitting in the dark. He looked around and started to walk forward when Donna shook her head no.

He backed up and saw the trip wires, so he stopped. He saw Jack, who had just gotten there before him. Jack whispered, "Don't move. You're standing on a detonator, and the charge is under the girls!"

Red whispered, "Where are these guys, Jack?"

"I heard you got the two upstairs, so my guess is there are two more goons and the senator. Looks like they are trying to get out of town, figuring this was going to blow us to hell."

"Can you get me off of this, Jack?"

"Yeah, I almost got it! Stand still." Jack took his military knife and reached under Red's boot and cut a lead. He said, "Step back slow."

Red said, "You had better be darn sure, Jack!"

"Back up now. It's on a delay and you just set it, so back up, Red!"

Jack dove forward and cut the lead to the explosive.

"Man, Jack, that was close!"

"Yeah, now let's get these girls out of here." They untied them and quickly moved them out of basement and onto the street.

"Where are the guys?" Jack asked.

"Roscoe and Ringo are down the street with some kids they pulled out of the hotel with Mrs. Thompson."

"Where is Gussie?"

"He's dead, Jack."

Terri said, "Where is my father?"

"I'm sorry, Terri."

"Oh God!" She broke down in tears.

Jack said, "Come on, we've got to move." They ran down the street.

Jack saw the other guys. They were waiting in the police station, which was a brick structure with few windows. Jack said, "You all stay here. I am going after them."

An older policeman was sitting in a chair and, in very good English, said, "They are headed to the airport."

Jack said, "What?"

"Local airport. They took a truck from town and are most likely driving to the airport."

"What direction?" Jack shouted.

"That way," he said and pointed south. "Here, take my police car." And he threw Jack the keys.

Jack jumped in the squad car and dropped it into gear and put it to the boards. He drove as fast as the car could go. The speedometer read 120 miles per hour. He neared the airport and spotted a small plane taxiing out from a hanger. As the plane turned toward the runway, Jack saw the senator seated in the copilot seat. Jack punched the throttle to the boards again and drove across the grass field. He slammed into the side of the plane. The plane spun around and flipped onto its side, tearing a wing off. Jack jumped out of the car with his gun drawn, while at the same time the first goon crawled out with his hands up and hollered said, "I am unarmed!"

Jack said, "That's your problem!" *Bang!* He shot him in the head. Then the second goon, who was in the pilot seat, came crawling out, trying to get his gun out of his jacket.

Jack put one between his eyes and said, "Too slow!" Jack grabbed the senator, who said, "You're not going to kill a US senator, son?"

"Oh, really," said Jack.

"They will hunt you for all your natural born days," he said with a cocky grin.

Jack said, "Give me the book, scumbag!"

"You're making a big mistake, son."

"Oh, am I, scumbag?"

"You will never get out of here alive!"

"Really. You know I have killed a lot of your special friends, now haven't I?"

"Yeah." He smirked. "And I have killed a lot of yours too!"

Jack said, "You piece of garbage! You still think you can threaten me?"

"I told you, son, they will hunt you!"

Jack said, "Sticks and stones. Sticks and stones," and pulled the trigger, but the gun did not fire!

The senator reached down and snatched the dead goon's gun on the ground and pointed it at Jack. He smirked again but then gasped. He shook, and blood started running from his mouth. He dropped the gun and fell face first and then Jack saw the throwing knife in his back. The book fell to Jack's feet, and he leaned down and picked it up.

He looked up again to see Ringo standing outside of the car that he had taken from town.

He said, "Jack?"

"Yeah, Ringo."

With tears in his eyes, he said, "They killed my friend, man. They killed Gussie!"

Jack said, "I know, man, I know."

Ringo walked over to join Jack, and they held on to each other as they walked to the car and drove away.

On the way back to town, there were police cars going by with their sirens blazing. They slowly drove with the windows down and the radio on. Ironically they heard the song that they use to sing in Vietnam when there was a fierce fire fight. It was the song by Dobie Grey, "Give Me the Beat Boys and save my soul. I want to get lost in your rock and roll and drift away." They both sang along when Jack took the book and gave it to Ringo.

He smiled and said, "This is a copy, isn't it?"

Jack smiled back and said, "Yeah, we know Gussie, and we know this is just a copy."

Ringo took the book and threw it out the window into the desert. It landed next to a cactus, and the wind blew the pages over one at a time.

The Beginning of the End

Thirty-five years later, Veterans Day, 2010

It was early afternoon, and the wind had slowed to a mild breeze. The sun was shone down on the well-kept lawn of Washington Square. The Vietnam Memorial was grand in the view of the first-time visitors to the site.

Polished stone with names of sons, fathers, husbands, and loved ones for the world to see.

Along the memorial were rows of personal items the families and friends of the fallen had left on the ground. Somehow these people felt connected to the now deceased soldiers when they left items and touched the engraved names.

A tall, slender, attractive, middle-aged woman was standing in front of a name her eyes were fixed upon it. She took a piece of paper, laid it across the engraved letters. and rubbed ever so gently with a pencil so the name would appear.

Standing next to her was a young man in his thirties. Tall, strong, handsome, he took her hand. "Mom," he said.

"Yeah, son," she responded with tears in her eyes.

"What kind of soldier was my father?"

She smiled as tears were streaming down her face. "The kind that would have loved you more than anything, that's what kind."

She then opened her purse and took out an old, leather, worn, pocket-type notebook with handwritten dates and some photographs and papers in it. She laid it down on the ground in front of the monument.

She then folded the paper with the name she had rubbed off with the pencil, and she knelt down and put the paper in the front cover. They turned and hugged each other and slowly walked along the memorial as she continued to weep. Her son held her hand as they walked back to the car.

It was evening just before sundown, and the grounds keeper was pushing a metal cart along the walkway, picking up all the items that were left at the base of the memorial. He picked up the book and brushed it off and opened the cover.

His English is not so good, so he put it in the cart with the rest of the items and headed to the storeroom where the items are kept. He asked his coworker, Mary, a retired school teacher, what was in the book. "Is it important," he said in thick Spanish accent.

He handed her the book, and she put down her coffee and opened the cover.

Her eyes were glued the pages as she began to read the contents. She remained silent as she read it page by page, looking at the occasional photographs that were put in between the pages. After several minutes of studying, she looked at the groundskeeper and said, "Important cannot describe what is in this book."

The groundskeeper smiled because he felt he had done a good deed by bringing this to her, rather than just storing it on the shelves with the rest of the items.

Mary took the book home at the end of the day. On her way home she picked up a newspaper to read after dinner. She looked on the front page and saw a photo and address of the newspaper office. She stopped by the local Federal Express office and filled out a parcel package slip, leaving the return address blank. She paid the clerk and handed him the package to mail. He smiled and dropped it in the chute to be shipped.

Friday, November 12, 2010, Washington Post, 9:00 a.m.

The package had arrived at the newspaper mailroom, and a young college student saw the name, Randolph Biggs, in bold letters. He told the mailroom supervisor, "Hey, I need to run this one. It's for Mr. Biggs!"

He nodded and said, "Go for it" to the kid as he was fumbled through a mountain of letters and never

turned to look at him. Out the door and into the eleva-
tor he went. His excitement built as he reached the top
floor. *Aw, finally I will see mahogany row and the great
Mr. Biggs, Chief Editor of the Post.* He approached the
large desk that was manned by an attractive woman
in her thirties who talking on the phone. He stopped
and smiled; she paused and put her hand on the phone.
"Yes, what is it?"

"I have a package for Mr. Biggs. Can I bring it
to him?"

She rolled her eyes and said, "If it's a thrill for you,
kid, go ahead," and she pushed the buzzer to open the
glass door. He headed down the hall. The phones were
ringing and the keyboards were clicking. The excitement of it all left him speechless. He reached the door
with a large, wooden sign that read: "Randolph Biggs,
Chief Editor."

Waiting outside the door, he found himself too
frightened to step in. He stood there mesmerized as he
watched the great Randolph Biggs read papers and sip
his morning coffee. After what seemed to be an eter-
nity, Randolph said from behind the paper, "Come on
in, kid, or are you going to just stare at me all day?"

The kid swallowed and stepped up to the desk and
said, "This came for you, sir. I thought it was important."

"Oh, you did. Well, thank you, young man," he said.

Randolph opened the package. He opened the book
and flipped through the pages. After reading a few
pages, he put his hand on his forehead and picked up
the phone. "Sarah, get me legal and all senior staff now!
My office now!"

He gingerly laid the book down on his desk and immediately turned, opened his liquor cabinet, and poured a glass of Irish whiskey for himself and one for the kid. Then he turned and gave one glass to the kid. He raised his glass up and said,

"Good God, do we have a story to tell!"